"Put me down, Blaise," she ordered.

"Why?" he asked, but did as she asked. "We're both consenting adults."

"You're consenting," she pointed out, her heart pounding hard. "I'm not. I'm past that."

He ran his finger along her lower lip. An involuntary tremor threatened to break loose, but Pat held onto control, willing herself to believe that he was planning on making love to the Hamilton jet, not her. This was not personal, she echoed over and over, but her body did not want to believe it and yearned for the promised excitement that existed just beyond his bedroom door.

He loomed over her, tall and broad-shouldered, standing bigger than life and filling out every space in her small hallway. "You're not past 'that'," he informed her, bending his head and kissing her softly. "You're not dead yet, are you?"

Like a flame, feelings of consuming passion swept over her, more fervent than any need she had ever known. . . .

WHAT ARE *LOVESWEPT* ROMANCES?

They are stories of true romance and touching emotion. We believe those two very important ingredients are constants in our highly sensual and very believable stories in the *LOVESWEPT* line. Our goal is to give you, the reader, stories of consistently high quality that may sometimes make you laugh, sometimes make you cry, but are always fresh and creative and contain many delightful surprises within their pages.

Most romance fans read an enormous number of books. Those they truly love, they keep. Others may be traded with friends and soon forgotten. We hope that each *LOVESWEPT* romance will be a treasure—a "keeper." We will always try to publish

LOVE STORIES YOU'LL NEVER FORGET
BY AUTHORS YOU'LL ALWAYS REMEMBER

The Editors

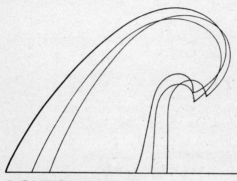

LOVESWEPT · 9

Marie Michael
December 32nd . . .
and Always

 BANTAM BOOKS · TORONTO · NEW YORK · LONDON · SYDNEY

*This book is dedicated
to the memory
of my mother,
a truly wonderful little
lady*

DECEMBER 32ND . . . AND ALWAYS
A Bantam Book / June 1983

LOVESWEPT and the wave device are trademarks of
Bantam Books, Inc.

ISBN 0-553-21608-2

Published simultaneously in the United States and Canada

---

*Bantam Books are published by Bantam Books, Inc. Its
trademark, consisting of the words "Bantam Books" and the
portrayal of a rooster, is Registered in U.S. Patent and Trademark Office and in other countries. Marca Registrada. Bantam
Books, Inc., 666 Fifth Avenue, New York, New York 10103.*

PRINTED IN THE UNITED STATES OF AMERICA

O   0 9 8 7 6 5 4 3 2 1

One

The first surprise was the roses on her desk.

The last time Patrissa Covington Hamilton had received roses was twelve years ago, on her eighth wedding anniversary. That was before Roger had gotten so caught up in his work.

But Roger had been gone for over a year now, taken from her just as she was approaching what she had always termed "the mellow years." When Pat blew out the forty candles on her birthday cake, she was far from able to relax in the comfortable companionship of the man she had been married to all her adult life. Instead, she faced the biggest challenge of her life. A challenge that had been handed to her by her husband on his deathbed—to complete his crowning achievement, to give wing to his impossible dream.

And what better person to have asked? Roger had always said he saw Pat as an extension of himself. But his work had clouded his vision and he had not seen how different from him his wife really was. But he had been right about one thing. He knew Pat was loyal enough to give it her all . . . and then some.

Indeed, his brothers, mother, and assorted other members of the family had gone from shaking their heads to looking at Pat as if she had lost her mind. The dream, they pointed out over and over again, would never get off the ground.

A good choice of words, she had thought at the time, because Roger's dream had involved a revolutionary airplane, lighter than what was out there now, its outer frame constructed of specially treated material, enabling it to get mileage like that of a heavy car of the fifties.

Her mind had been on the thousand and one obstacles facing her when she walked into her office on the second floor of the plant located outside Albuquerque, New Mexico. She was startled by the sight of those two dozen roses, an exquisite splash of brilliance in the otherwise colorless and severely decorated office. What was this? she wondered. A peace offering? Or a bribe? What were Roger's two brothers up to now?

Pat turned to the tall, powerful-looking Zuni Indian who had been her husband's right hand at the plant for fifteen years. Roger had given him a job when no one else wanted to take a chance on a man recently out of prison. Sam White Horse had been a little high-spirited in his youth, but he had given Roger two hundred percent of his loyalty for his kindness, and he had transferred his silent devotion to Pat when she had assumed the mantle of chairman of the board. It was he who kept her abreast of everything, both inside the plant and out. Sam knew everything that was going on or about to go on. Everything, it seemed, but the origin of the roses.

"There's no card," Pat said, still staring at the flowers. "I wonder what those two are up to."

Sam obviously knew whom she was talking about. "They aren't the type to send flowers at all," Sam observed. "And if they did, it would be chrysanthemums. They last longer."

Pat smiled, lighting up her slightly rounded face. "You've got that right." She bent her head to smell the flowers. The fragrance of the recently opened buds was heavenly.

"But if they didn't send them, who did?" she asked.

"I did."

That was the second surprise.

Pat spun toward the voice. The sight of the tall figure in the doorway virtually destroyed her composure. Her soft brown eyes grew wide, and her hand unconsciously flew to her head to make sure that the fashionably arranged honey-brown hair was not mussed and that all the pins were in place.

"Blaise," she said in an audible whisper that made Sam look at his diminutive boss with an arched brow.

Nervousness took hold of Pat. Her insides quivered as her eyes swept over the tall, almost unbearably handsome man who stood in the doorway of her office. Just behind him, Pat could see Alice, her secretary, peering hungrily at Blaise's back.

He hadn't changed.

Pat had first seen him twenty-one years ago, and except for the gray touches at his temples, he hadn't changed at all. Except, perhaps, that he had grown handsomer. Dear God, what was she thinking of? She tried to rally herself mentally. She was an old married—no, widowed—woman. This fluster she was experiencing was something teenage girls felt at seeing their idol up close. No one else had ever had this effect on her, not even Roger, not the first time he had taken her into his arms or the first time he had made love to her. What was the matter with her? Pat wondered, color rising to her face. She thanked God she had a healthy tan to hide that betraying red.

Where was her easygoing, laid-back manner now, just when she needed it? she thought frantically. Blaise Hamilton was a world traveler, used to the company of the highest run of society. She couldn't behave like a schoolgirl in front of him. After all, she was Patrissa Covington Hamilton, chairman of the board, a wealthy lady. . . .

She found herself staring at the broad shoulders beneath the camel-colored, custom-made suit jacket he was wearing. He still had a trim waist, she caught herself thinking, even after all these years of rich living.

Blaise strode forward and took her hand in his, kissing it lightly in the continental style, making Alice sigh as she looked on.

"Lady Pat," he said fondly, using the name he had given her at their first meeting, when Roger's father had announced their engagement. "You've managed to keep your incredible figure. Matter of fact," he said, his startling blue eyes seeming to drink in the sight of her, "I think you've improved on it." He smiled down at her, a wide, white smile that was framed beguilingly against an olive complexion. "I wouldn't have believed that was possible," he said in a rich baritone voice that surrounded her.

Pat suddenly remembered the silent figure to her left. "Sam, I'd like you to meet Blaise Hamilton, Roger's cousin," she said, satisfied that her voice did not quaver and betray her. "Blaise, this is Sam White Horse. He—runs everything here," she said pleasantly, smiling at the tall Indian, who was casually dressed in comparison to Blaise.

Sam merely nodded at Blaise, and shook the man's hand only after it was thrust toward him. Pat could see that Sam was sizing Blaise up. She knew that her tremulous reaction to Blaise's sudden appearance was evident to Sam.

"Very pleased to meet you," Blaise said in his genial manner, then looked back at Pat. "How are you?" he asked, and the question seemed to ask so much more.

"Well," she replied. "I'm well." She put her hand on the corner of her desk. "What brings you here?" she asked, trying to sound casual. She had no business reacting to him like this. It was so . . . so silly.

"I'm here to help," he said simply. "Here for as long as I'm needed." He gestured toward a suitcase by the door.

Was he here for a visit? she wondered. If so, whom was he visiting? He didn't get along with the other members of the family. As a matter of fact, when she had first met him, he was called "the black sheep of the family" by a very disapproving Mother Rose. He and Roger had gotten on well enough, but Roger was gone, and besides, Blaise hadn't even come to the funeral.

His words suddenly sank in.

"Help?" she echoed dumbly.

"Yes," he said smoothly. "Help."

"Who?" she asked, drawing her brows together.

"You."

"Me?"

What did he mean? Blaise was into high finance, dealing with the powers behind heads of governments, using his extreme charm to wheel and deal—and he wasn't above having a good time while he was at it. Pat had read that he and a contessa from somewhere had been discovered wading in one of the fountains in Rome at four in the morning. With anyone else, it would have been a whispered scandal. With Blaise, all that came of the event were patient, good-natured smiles—and the contessa's broken heart in the long run, Pat guessed.

"Aunt Delia wrote that Rose has managed to turn the family against you, even Sara and Bucky," he said, referring to her two college-aged children. "She thought you might like someone in your corner besides a feisty, eighty-year-old lady, bound to a wheelchair."

Oh yes, Aunt Delia. Pat had forgotten that Blaise was her favorite and that she highly approved of his high-spirited ways, while the rest of the family, entrenched in their "traditions," had been happy to see Blaise leave shortly after Pat's wedding.

"I would have been here sooner," Blaise continued, "but it took some time for her letter to reach me. I move around quite a bit."

"I bet you do," Pat said before she could stop herself.

Blaise threw back his head and laughed a deep,

resonant laugh that could bring about a smile from a statue, Pat had once thought. "Still the spunky, outspoken girl," Blaise remarked approvingly. He took her hand again, smiling down into her face as he towered over her by a good foot. "I'm glad," he said warmly.

Pat cleared her throat. "I'm hardly a girl," she reminded him.

"To me you'll always be a girl," he said easily. "A beautiful, blushing girl in a pale blue dress," he added, referring to the first time he had seen her.

"I don't blush," she said, trying to keep her voice emotionless, mindful of the fact that Sam was still in the room.

"You did when I danced with you," Blaise reminded her.

He remembered that? she thought in surprise. Did he keep a catalog of all the women he had encountered in his life? She decided the topic was best dropped. Her eyes fell to the suitcase.

"Where are you staying?" she asked.

"As I remember it, your house is a sprawling hacienda with a great number of rooms in it."

She stared at him in disbelief. Was he planning on moving in?

"Now, if I'm going to help," he said, his arms crossed over his chest, "I should stick close by."

"How close?" she asked archly.

"That, Lady Pat, depends entirely upon you and your needs," he said, leaning forward slightly.

On the surface, the sentence was innocent enough, but Pat knew Blaise's reputation and that there was simply nothing innocent about him. His meaning was all too clear.

"I, um, don't think—" she began.

"Of course," Blaise continued loftily, as if she hadn't attempted to say anything, "Aunt Rose might not approve."

Pat's face tightened. She knew he was goading her, but he was right. Mother Rose wouldn't approve. But Pat took pleasure in deliberately making Mother Rose disapprove. Besides, in the long run, there was nothing wrong with having a houseguest, even if the children were away at school. There was Angelica to chaperon them. Chaperon. Really, Pat, you're beginning to sound like you're a hundred years old, she chided herself. Besides, nothing would happen. Here Blaise was offering her the support she so desperately craved from the family, and she was acting as if he might be offering her poison.

"You're welcome to stay at the house," she said firmly.

Blaise smiled, as if he had known the outcome all along. "Angelica still there?"

"Angelica will always be there," Pat said, surprised that he remembered the housekeeper's name and wondering if he took her hidden meaning.

Blaise's deep smile told her that her words were thoroughly digested. "Fine woman, Angelica. Well," he said "let me get settled and then pay my respects to Delia. I'll be back to take you to dinner," he promised as he began to leave the room, pausing at the doorway to retrieve his suitcase.

"But—"

Pat was about to protest that she had dinner at the office these days, working until well into the night, but Blaise seemed not to hear her as he shook Sam's hand again and then winked over his shoulder before leaving.

"Do you good to leave on time for a change," Sam said after Blaise had gone.

"Taken up mind reading, Sam?" she asked. "There's much too much work to do—"

"You plan to do it all in one night?" Sam asked mildly.

"No," she laughed, "but—"

"So there's no harm in letting the midnight oil go out for a change, is there?" Sam asked as he walked to the door.

"No," Pat said slowly, "I suppose not. . . ."

But as Sam left the room, Pat wasn't so sure.

She sat down at her desk. Somehow the urgency that had powered each morning since Roger's death had faded temporarily as she tried to assimilate what had just taken place. Blaise was back, disrupting her life the way he had when he had first entered it. But she was a lot older now, and supposedly wiser. She had been a wife, a mother, a chief accountant, and now she was the apparent backbone of Hamilton Enterprises. A lot had happened in her life since she had first set disbelieving eyes on Blaise. Why did he ruin her well-earned self-confidence with just a smile?

Until she had first seen him, looking at her across a crowded dance floor with those penetrating eyes of his, Pat had thought men who looked like Blaise Hamilton were only beautifully penned princes in fairy tales or romantic dreams. She had been on Roger's arm at that moment, being introduced to a distant family friend, when she had first caught sight of Blaise watching her. His overpowering masculine appeal had made her catch her breath and forget all the polite words she was supposed to say, and then she had felt like an idiot when Roger's friend stood waiting for a reply to some question or other.

She wasn't that way normally. Patrissa Covington had been named after her mother, Melissa, and her father, Patrick, who had wanted to give their first and, as it turned out, only child a name as unique as they felt she was. She was an equal composite of both parents, inheriting her mother's charm and good humor and her father's brains and good looks, although for a while it had looked as if she might stay an ugly duckling forever. She had been an awkward, plain child, so she had honed her sense of humor and developed a knack of listening that endeared her to almost everyone she met.

When nature finally woke up and fulfilled the promise that had been hinted at when Pat was a child, her enchanting exterior befit the inner person, making Pat Covington's company the type to be sought out by everyone. That was what had attracted Roger to her in the first place. She had listened to all his dreams, never scoffing at the things he proposed, things that could, as yet, not even be framed on a drawing board. She had been the initial drive that had set him going.

The children had arrived quickly, and Pat had devoted herself to being a mother during their formative years, loving her children, yet yearning to get back to Roger's work world again. When she did get back, it wasn't the same.

Oh, the people around the plant were the same crowd as in the beginning, and their loyalty had grown, if anything. But Roger was different. She was no longer the first person in his life. He had taken on a mistress—his work. He was in love with his planes, and the money and fame he had gleaned from producing them was not enough. He was forever improving the planes, forever tinkering with their insides. He was a chairman of the board who arrived each morning in shirtsleeves, ready to pitch in with his men, knowing every detail of what was going on.

There was precious little room for Pat in this life. Another woman might have retreated, but not Pat. She was a survivor and she hung on, making the best of the situation, getting herself as involved as she could in the large company that had sprung up under her husband's hand. The work kept her from realizing just how disappointed she was with her life.

That was the word. Disappointed. She was not sure just what it was she had expected from married life. Certainly a closeness and an interdependency, but she had found that for only a few years—in the beginning, when Roger had counted on her enthusiastic support.

Pat had also expected—romance. Silly, wasn't it? she thought. She had hoped for blissfully romantic, candlelit evenings when her pulse would race madly at the mere sight of her husband, at the mere touch of his hand. But, quite honestly, that had never been there. She loved Roger dearly. He was a good, honest, kind man without a mean bone in his body. And that, she told herself time and again, should have been enough for her. And it would have been, perhaps, had Blaise never entered her life.

And now he was back. She pursed her lips,

straightening her shoulders as if getting ready to do battle. With determination, she pushed all thoughts of the man out of her head and marched outside to immerse herself in the noisy, demanding business that existed right outside her door.

Two

Pat had almost given in to the urge to dash home at lunchtime and change, but another of the Eagle's components had failed an important stress test, and Pat's attention had been called to the emergency. They were two months short of their self-imposed deadline—December 31st—and there was still so much to do, so many details to see to, not the least of which were the pending court battle and Hamilton Enterprises' dwindling supply of money.

All these thoughts were racing through Pat's mind as she hurried back to her office, hoping to have at least enough time to comb her hair and freshen up her makeup before Blaise arrived.

Deep in the pit of her stomach, a knot was tightening.

But he was in her office, waiting for her, sitting behind the desk as if he belonged there. Pat's eyes narrowed. Did Blaise have designs on Hamilton Enterprises? Was that the real reason for his presence? Or had he made peace with the others and been enlisted to get Pat to stop her "foolishness" and give up Roger's project?

Pat was beginning to feel that she couldn't trust anyone, and the sensation was new to her. She did not like being on her guard so much. Even here at the plant, where she supposedly had everyone's support, she caught herself wondering about this employee's loyalty, or that one's. It was all making her very tired. That was probably what Sam had seen when he had urged her to go out.

Blaise had changed, she observed. He was wearing a pearl-gray suit with a light blue shirt. A gray tie completed the picture. He looked as if he had stepped out of a Brooks Brothers ad in the magazine section of the *Times*. Her own two-piece, tailored outfit looked out of place as she vainly tried to envision herself on his arm.

Then she noticed a garment bag on the wine-colored leather sofa in the corner. "Are you expecting to get very dirty during dinner?" she asked dryly, nodding toward it.

He smiled. Why did that smile dazzle her so? she demanded of herself. "I asked Angelica what sort of outfit you'd feel comfortable in, dining out with an admirer."

Pat felt her throat go dry. "What made you do a thing like that?" she asked, forcing herself to go over to the garment bag and open it, just to have something to do to avoid his eyes.

"Well," Blaise said, and began ticking the points off on his fingers, "number one, according to Delia, you're working yourself into a frazzle, keeping long hours, so I knew you wouldn't be home to change, and I knew that most ladies don't like to eat out in their work clothes. Number two, I am an admirer of yours. I always have been," he said significantly in a tone that was half a note lower than his usual voice, "and number three, Angelica doesn't utter more than three words at a time except under torture, so I knew she wouldn't repeat any part of my statement. There, does that cover all bases?" he asked genially, coming toward her.

"Quite," Pat said. Part of her wanted to retreat for some unknown reason, and the rest of her, her stubborn side, told her to stand fast—which she did.

She opened the bag to find a pretty navy and white wraparound dress with a soft floral design. She hadn't worn it in years. What made Angelica pick this? she wondered, glancing up suspiciously at Blaise, who smiled at her innocently. "Angelica didn't pick this out," she declared. "You did."

"She showed me where your clothes were," he said. "That counts for something."

Pat sighed. Well, there was no harm in it, she supposed. "Wait here, I'll be right back," she said, stepping into the adjoining office, which had been hers before Roger had died and she had inherited the bigger office with her new title.

"Need any help with those buttons?" Blaise offered considerately.

She glanced down at the simple shirtwaist she was wearing. "The buttons are in front," she pointed out.

"Yes," he said, "I know."

Pat was more than a little unsettled as she shut the door firmly behind her.

He took her to one of Albuquerque's most elegant restaurants, where the plush decor and subdued lighting bespoke intimacy and romance. But Pat's mind was occupied by problems at the plant and the upcoming court battle contesting Roger's sanity at the time that he "chained" her to this commitment. Then she looked into Blaise's intense eyes. The butterflies in her stomach turned into Hamilton jets and kept growing, though she kept reminding herself that she was a mature woman and that he, after all, was merely a man.

Merely a man. That was like saying that the Grand Canyon was just a hole in the ground, or that the Taj Mahal was just a building. Roger had once told her, with obvious affection for his cousin, that while Blaise was regarded as a black sheep by the family, his rugged, almost perfect good looks had made him a subject of female prey since the first grade. A giggling, pigtailed girl had eluded her mother and followed him home, hiding in the back seat of the family car when Blaise's governess had picked him up. He had been a beautiful child and had grown up to become probably the handsomest man most people had ever seen.

"Well, it's been a long time," Pat said finally, hating the stilted way that sounded. She had hostessed huge parties for Roger, keeping conversation flowing among scores of people. Why was she so tongue-tied now? She resented Blaise for the effect he had on her. But then, no woman except for Mother Rose could resent Blaise for long. He had that inordinate charm about him that made women from six to sixty forgive him countless trespasses.

"Ten years," Blaise said. "And you've gotten more beautiful."

"And you've gotten even more honey on your tongue," she countered, toying with her wineglass.

"Honey is to catch flies," Blaise said. "I'm not after flies."

"Oh?" she asked, cocking her head. "Just what is it you *are* after?" There was no coyness in her voice. She wanted a straight answer.

He looked as if he were about to respond, then hesitated. Finally he replied, "Right now, to help you."

"Why?"

"Why not?" he said with a guileless smile.

"I asked first," she persisted. She didn't want to play games. The project was too important.

"I believe in fighting for the underdog—no physical comparison intended," he said mischievously, his eyes playing with the décolletage created by the crisscross pattern of the wraparound dress. The fullness of her breasts was emphasized by the tininess of her waist, a feature she was proud of after bearing two children. A feature that she had earned from hours of rigorous exercise at the gym—another method of filling her lonely life.

"None taken," Pat said, a smile creeping across her lips.

"Good, you're smiling. I always liked your smile."

"When did you have time to notice it?" Pat asked in surprise. Since that time when she was eighteen, she had seen him only a handful of times, always at family gatherings, never for long. In a way, that had been merciful, for his presence had unsettled her, despite her so-called happy marriage. He seemed to carry the promise of excitement within him, awakening Pat's nearly forgotten unfulfilled dreams.

"You'd be surprised," he said in a whisper, making her feel as if she were eavesdropping on a private conversation between Blaise and himself.

"You're being polite," she said.

"I'm being honest."

Pat shifted uncomfortably and was grateful that the waitress chose that instant to come by for their dessert order.

But soon they were alone again, sitting at a table that was, for the moment, their own inviolate world. Two candles stood on either side of the tiny flower arrangement on the lace-covered table and their yellow flames flickered hypnotically.

Into this mesmerizing moment floated Blaise's voice. "If I have any regrets in my life," he said softly, "it's that I let a delightful eighteen-year-old pixie slip through my fingers."

Pat jerked her head up. Oh no, he wasn't catching her with any well-rehearsed lines. If he thought he was descending on some love-starved widow who would fall into his lap at the sound of a few carefully chosen words, he was in for a rude awakening.

"I was never in your fingers," she said pointedly, her voice firm as she looked straight into his eyes. She was a big girl now, and not to be taken for a fool by anyone.

"That's because I didn't try." His candor took her totally aback.

Pat's eyes narrowed. "I was in love with Roger," she said sharply.

"Nobody was fonder of Roger than I was, but he wasn't a romantic. He was a meat-and-potatoes man, and you, Lady Pat, deserved filet mignon and gypsy violins. You deserved someone who would pick flowers to tuck behind your ear."

She studied him coldly. "Well, you're certainly not the shy, retiring type."

"You wouldn't have liked me if I was," he said simply.

Her brows shot up. "Rather sure of yourself, aren't you?"

"I just know women," he said, reaching for her hand.

She pulled it back, annoyed. "Why, you egotist. You think you're so special that—"

"You tell me," he said softly, touching the outline of her face with the back of his fingertips, gliding them sensuously along her cheek. "I know I could make you feel as special as you really are."

He did know how to turn a phrase against a person, Pat thought, annoyed with him yet strangely intrigued. She felt as if her wit had been yanked away as she searched for a reply. Eventually, almost grudgingly, she said, "You certainly don't leave much room for argument."

"I never argue with a beautiful girl," he corrected.

"I told you before," she said firmly, "I'm not a girl."

He leaned forward, and the flames from the candles danced in his eyes. "Inside every young girl is a woman and inside every woman is a young girl, yearning for romance and eternal love."

"Well, thank you, Dr. Hamilton, for your brilliant thesis, but all that I yearn for is to finish Roger's project and begin to turn out those Eagles. As a matter of fact, with Mother Rose so staunchly against me, nothing in the world would give me greater pleasure," she said, accepting the ice-cream sundae the waitress placed in front of her.

"Oh, I think something else can," Blaise told her with a smile, "but for now, on to your quest."

"Are you serious?" Pat studied him, her brown eyes revealing nothing of her anxiety. "About helping me with the project, I mean," she clarified before he could read any other meaning into her words.

"Really," he said.

And as she looked into his eyes, eyes that normally held the look of a mischievous boy, she saw that he was telling the truth. Either that, or he was an awfully good liar—which he probably was, she thought, considering the types of people he encountered in his work.

"What can I do to help?" he asked, his hand slipping across the table to grasp hers. She had been the recipient of this friendly gesture countless times. But now it sent a shiver down her spine, a warm, tingling, delicious shiver that a woman her age and in her position had no business feeling, she told herself.

"You wouldn't have an unlimited source of money, would you?" she asked laughing.

He responded in kind. "No, not in my pocket—but if money is your problem, I know I can help."

"Money is only one of my problems, but we're not talking five or ten thousand dollars, Blaise," Pat said earnestly, the thought of the eventual hopelessness of the situation wearying her. She allowed herself to think of the venture only one step at a time. One test at a time. They worked on a tight, tight budget, with many of the workers taking a cut in pay, turning the project into a labor of love, risking their necks along with hers.

"Madam, I never talk about five or ten thousand dollars. I stopped thinking that small a long time ago," he said with a wink. Anyone else saying this would have sounded like a braggart, but Blaise was reporting the simple truth.

"I need someone to finance this," she said honestly.

"What about Roger's money?" he asked, taking a sip of his wine.

"It has all been reinvested in the company," she said. "I've sold nearly everything of value. The cars are all gone, except for Roger's beloved Mercedes. I'd hate to sell the house, but . . ." She let her voice trail off. If she had to, she would.

Blaise patted her hand affectionately. "You hang on to that house, Lady Pat. A princess should always have a castle, even if it doesn't have a moat."

"Before you jump into this, oh gallant knight," she said dryly, "don't you think you should know exactly what you're championing? A lot of people who should know say this isn't going to work."

He looked into her eyes, catching her off guard and making all her practical, careful words stick in her throat. His blue eyes smiled at her as they washed over her warmly. "What do you say?" he asked.

"Roger knew everything there was to know about flying. He had faith that this thing would work. A I have faith in Roger," she said simply but firmly.

"So it shall be written, so it shall be done," Blaise said with a flourish of his hand. "Yul Brynner, *The Ten Commandments*," he added with a grin.

"Does that mean that if the plane lands in the ocean, you'll part the waters for me?"

"That might require a little more money than I can raise quickly, but I'd give it my best shot," he promised.

"Well, don't worry about it. That won't be necessary." Her tone was serious once again. "But I would appreciate any financial assistance on the Eagle's behalf."

"That's what I'm here for, Lady Pat. Of course you've got a deal." His level gaze held hers for a moment. Then a playful glint crept into his expression. "Well, now that we have that settled," Blaise said, "how about going dancing with me?"

"Oh no," Pat protested, glancing at her watch. "I couldn't."

"Sure you could," he insisted. "All you do is mold your body to mine and I'll take care of the rest."

"I'm sure you would," she said, eyeing him, "but body molding is another thing I'm not into."

"Another thing?" he echoed. "What else aren't you 'into'?"

"Dancing."

"As I remember, you dance very well," he said.

"But—" Her strength to resist was beginning to fade. Perhaps it would be fun to be in his arms—safely dancing, of course.

"I didn't get where I am today by taking no for an answer," Blaise said, rising and taking her hand. "Waitress," he called, "check, please."

Within minutes, Pat found herself whisked off to a popular night spot and enfolded in Blaise's strong arms, the envy of every woman she drifted by.

The song that floated around them suddenly made her smile: "I know you, I walked with you once upon a dream." Yes, the memory of their first dance resembled a dream now. Blaise had indeed looked like a prince when he had swept her away from Roger, claiming a waltz with his cousin-to-be. There had been a strange, electric charge between them, which Pat had cautiously chalked up to the two glasses of wine she had drunk earlier in the evening.

They had hardly spoken, or at least she hadn't. He had murmured polite words, but his eyes—his eyes had said something entirely different, something terribly unsettling. She had felt more . . . intimate was the word, she supposed now, with Blaise in those three minutes than she had with Roger in the three years they had known each other.

When the dance was over, she had been almost relieved to return to Roger's side. But there had been a sense of disappointment as well. She had shrugged off the disturbing feeling, although she had been aware of Blaise's eyes following her throughout the evening.

• • •

"Remember the first time we danced together?" Blaise asked, his words touching her hair. The feel of his closeness excited her.

"My engagement party," she said, once she was sure her voice would not betray her. Had he read her mind?

"Yes, when that lucky son of a gun swept you away in front of all those approving people," he said wryly.

"You never liked the Hamilton family, did you?" Pat asked as he whirled her around the floor. Another song was playing now, its beat getting under her skin and making her feel wonderfully alive.

She was enjoying herself, actually enjoying herself, without any worry lines tugging at her brow. It was delightful. She had heard that Blaise had this effect on women. For what it was worth, she was grateful. But as to any other effects he might have, well, she was too wise to be caught up in that! She tried not to stare at his dark head while she waited for him to reply.

"Delia's a sharp little lady. Wouldn't want to match wits with her. And Roger was a good sort, but as for the rest," his face clouded slightly, as if he was recounting hidden memories, "icebergs, all of them."

"Even your parents?" she asked, surprised at the bitterness of his words.

"Worst offenders of all," he said without emotion. "Hardly saw them long enough to learn their names." Blaise's shining eyes examined her more closely, and he cocked his head slightly. The gesture made him look even more appealing, if that was possible. "I often wondered how someone like you managed to find her way into the Ice Dynasty. Someone so warm and vibrant, so full of life."

"How could you possibly know all that?" she asked, allowing herself to go along with the game she was sure he was playing, wondering how far he intended to take it. "You were hardly around."

"Oh, Lady Pat," he teased, "one doesn't have to live in someone's pocket to know all about them. There's such a thing as feelings and instincts. Mine are very keen when it comes to the ladies."

"I know," Pat said with an indulgent smile.

"Oh, and how do you know?" he laughed, echoing her previous tone. He seemed to take delight in this little game.

Pat found his company refreshing and charming, and she could easily see why he was such a favorite with women. While his looks were almost overwhelming, it was his charm that managed to disarm people.

"I've read about you. *Time* and *Life* and all the big magazines at one time or another have mentioned your terribly important, hush-hush transactions . . . the beautiful women you've been involved with," she added with a smile, waiting to hear his reply to that.

"Ah, a fan," he said easily. "So, you've been following my humble life. I'm flattered."

"Humble, huh! Anyone who can get an audience with those sheiks in the oil cartel just by appearing at their hotel while they're squabbling over the price of oil *and* be invited back to all their countries as, I believe the term was, an 'honored guest' has left that 'humble' bit far behind," she said. "Tell me, is it true that one of them offered you a harem girl of your very own?" She innocently looked up at his face.

"No, not one of them," Blaise said, then paused before he added, "three of them."

"Did you bring them along?" Pat teased.

He shook his head solemnly. "They were dressed too draftily for this part of the country. I left them with the customs agent at the airport. I believe he's still searching them for hidden contraband— and having the time of his life," he said with a twinkle in his eye.

Pat laughed, feeling blissfully younger than she had in years. "You've never grown up, have you?" she asked.

"What was there to grow up to?" he countered. "Wearing long faces like the others? No, I believe in grabbing everything life has to offer and enjoying it—or else, why grab?"

The band had stopped playing and Pat suddenly realized that they were the only ones on the floor. She had gotten so caught up in Blaise that she had created her own music in her head. With a slight, embarrassed laugh, she nodded toward the table.

"I think we'd better sit down before everyone starts staring."

"If they do, it'll be at you," he said simply, his voice silky. "Have I told you that you look beautiful tonight?" he asked, holding the brocade chair for her.

"No," she answered, feeling the nervous flutter return. She was all right while they were bantering, but he kept turning the conversation and his wonderful eyes back to her and making her feel so unsure of herself. It was all such nonsense.

"Well, then I must be slipping. Either that, or you've managed to dazzle me so much that you've made me forget my manners."

"I sincerely doubt that anyone could dazzle you to the extent that you'd forget *anything*," Pat said, then put up her hand. "And I'm not fishing for another compliment, so you can relax. I'm an old family friend, remember?"

"I'm not the one who's tense," he pointed out, and she shifted in her seat. "And you're hardly old," he said softly, his eyes seeming to take in every part of her.

Pat had always taken care of herself, watched her weight, kept up with the latest styles. And she had done it for herself, not in order to parade before chattering women at a garden club or to play the femme fatale at the parties she and Roger had thrown. She had thought of herself as just a person, a capable, mature person, not as a feminine entity. Yet she saw the latter reflected in Blaise's eyes, and the image almost . . . pleased her.

"I'm nearly forty-one," she said.

Blaise clutched at his heart and looked at her wide-eyed. "And you made it here without your wheelchair?"

Pat felt a giggle break loose and immediately fought to control it as a deep smile took possession of her lips. She hadn't giggled in years.

"You ninny, don't you know that the best is yet to be?" he asked fondly, and he would have looked serious had it not been for the mischievous gleam in his eye.

"You sound like a commercial," she said. "I've been married, I'm widowed, my children are grown and, at the moment, against me, more engrossed in money, it seems, than in the ideals Roger and I tried to instill in them—" She was about to say that the best part of her life was over, but Blaise didn't let her.

"Don't you see, you're a much more fascinating woman now than you were at your junior prom," he insisted, taking her hand. The atmosphere had suddenly become very intimate. "And like the commercial, you're not getting older, you're getting better."

"At what?" she asked with a touch of bitterness, thinking of all the obstacles she faced. "At losing?"

His finger gently traced the outline of her lips. "At a lot of things, I'd wager."

The candles on their table winked and blinked a bit brighter for a moment as Pat tried to free herself of the spell that was being cast. "I think it's getting late," she said with effort. "I do have to be up early tomorrow."

Blaise nodded and reached for his wallet. "Of course, Cinderella," he said, glancing at his watch, "although we still have a few hours before the coach becomes a pumpkin."

"They don't make pumpkins like they used to," Pat said, rising. "This one's got a shorter time limit on it." He helped her on with her fur stole. "I suppose this isn't what you're used to," she apologized, thinking of the glamorous women he squired about, sharing their company until the wee hours of the morning—the time she usually got up to start her day.

"No," he confessed with a warm smile, "it's not.

You're unique." He placed his hand against the small of her back as he guided her out to the car.

She wasn't sure how he meant that, and she suddenly realized that he would be coming home with her. The thought created a prickling sensation in her hands, which she tried to ignore.

Blaise merely smiled at her as he ushered her into the back seat of his chauffeured limousine.

Three

Blaise must have sensed her uneasiness. All the way home he asked questions about her work and the problems she was encountering. Safely nestled in the subject that dominated her life, Pat became animated and clearly defined the predicament as it stood at the moment, tossing off technical terms that once would have boggled her mind. But she had thrown herself into the task that Roger had left, armed with tenacity and a huge willingness to learn.

At Blaise's insistence, she gave him a capsulized version of her life in the past twenty years, bringing him up to date just as they reached her front door.

"You make it sound as if the plant and its products became Roger's whole life," Blaise commented, taking the key from her and opening the front door of her sprawling hacienda, which stood isolated on five acres.

"They did," Pat said honestly, going in and finding to her relief that Angelica had left the lights on in the spacious living room. Without thinking, Pat kicked off her shoes at the door, as was her custom, letting the thick pile of the freshly shampooed, cream-colored rug caress her tired feet. She looked up to find Blaise staring at her. She suddenly felt tiny next to him—and very, very vulnerable. It was just her imagination running away with her, she told herself. She was just tired, that was all.

Blaise shook his head as he closed the door softly behind him. "Poor old Roger. What a fool," he said almost under his breath.

"What?" Pat stopped in her tracks and turned to face Blaise.

"I said he was a fool," Blaise repeated more audibly. "To be so wrapped up in his work that he didn't see what he was allowing to go to waste right in his own home."

"Blaise, you've been wonderful for my ego," Pat began, walking over to the huge glass doors that led out to the terrace. She pulled the ceiling-to-floor drapes with a decisive, swift motion. "But you needn't waste your words on me. I don't feel cheated—"

"Don't you?" Blaise asked, coming toward her.

She realized as she turned to face him that he had taken off his tie and had undone the three top buttons of his shirt. A light layer of downy, dark hair was exposed. She caught herself wondering, just for a moment, what he would look like in swimming trunks. Most men looked passably well in three-piece suits but were a terrible disappointment in swimsuits. Roger had been athletic-looking when they were first married, but as the years had passed and his involvement with work grew, he had neglected himself. Her husband had eventually joined the ranks of flabby-bodied men whose trousers hung loosely behind them while almost straining against a little round belly in front, gained from eating the wrong foods on the run. Somehow, Pat instinctively knew that Blaise offered no such disappointment.

He whispered again, "Don't you feel cheated?"

She shrugged indifferently and responded to his question. "Just by the fact that he's gone, of course. Even though he wasn't here that often, I do miss him. And at the office, I still expect him to come marching through that door, dirty shirt-sleeves rolled up to his elbows, talking excitedly, trying to tell me how he improved on his line of planes." She sat down on the long blue and white sofa, looking up absently at the original impressionist painting that hung above it.

Unconsciously, she began to massage her feet. Blaise sat next to her.

"What's the matter?" he asked, looking at her hands as she rubbed her toes.

"It's my feet," Pat said, a little embarrassed. "I don't think they enjoyed this evening as much as the rest of me. I haven't been dancing in a long time," she confessed.

"Here," Blaise offered, drawing her feet onto his lap, "let me."

"No," she protested, trying to pull back, but he held firm.

"I promise I won't take them away," he told her as he began to knead.

Despite herself, Pat liked the wonderfully relax-

ing effect of his fingers as they methodically mas-
saged away the ache in her small feet. It felt
marvelous. Too marvelous, she realized, suddenly
drawing back and sitting up on her knees.

Blaise merely grinned.

"Roger really did have a very ingenious mind,"
she said, nervously retreating to the topic of her
husband. "I don't think his family appreciated
that."

Blaise nodded his dark head slightly. "I don't
think his family is capable of appreciating anything except more money." His eyes seemed to
pull her closer and make her feel totally exposed
before him. "So I take it you were happy with
him."

"Yes," Pat answered softly. Well, she had been,
even though at times she had been jealous of his
work's claim on him. Although he forgot her birth-
days and anniversaries, Roger could remember all
the parts of any plane he manufactured. Still, she
had loved him, right up to the end, and her loyalty
to him was unswerving.

"How happy?" Blaise pressed.

"Blaise, if you came here expecting to find a
frustrated, unhappy widow who would throw herself into the arms of the first man who offered her
sympathetic words . . ." she began, her annoyance showing.

But his smile erased the rest of her words. "I
came expecting to find the same pluck I always
saw in you and I'm not disappointed. I think I
would have been disappointed if you had knuck-
led under to Aunt Rose and given up the plant.
I'm glad to see you're still 'dynamite,' " he said
fondly.

She looked at him in surprise. How had he known her nickname? Pat's friends had called her that in high school and the name still aptly described her. She was petite and lithe—compact, she liked to put it—but she always made a difference when she became involved in something.

"How did you know my nickname?" Pat couldn't help asking.

"I know a lot of things about you. I made it a point to know."

"In between the harem girls and wading in the fountain with the contessa?" she asked, amused.

"In between everything," he said.

"Then why didn't you come to the funeral?" She remembered looking for his face at the time, feeling sure he would come to pay his respects rather than just send a wire of condolences and a flower arrangement. She realized now that unconsciously she had wanted him there to support her. Somehow, she had instinctively known that he would have been on her side.

"I wasn't sure that you needed me then," he said honestly.

"Well, I did," she answered, being more frank with him than she thought she should be.

"I realize that now," he replied. "Delia's letter took me to task for that."

"Delia's been wonderful," Pat said, "but she's somewhere in her late eighties, I think, and I don't want to tax her with any of my problems."

"You don't have to say anything to her. She's a sharp cookie. Has her fingers on the pulse of everything." He smiled. "She's kind of what I imagine you'll be like in another fifty years."

Pat realized that he had taken her hand in

his. Moreover, his other arm had slipped around her shoulders. She was surrounded. A tightness gripped her throat. She had to get up. She had no business being here alone with him like this, feeling as nervous as a teenager in the presence of the school "hunk." The thought made her smile. She had not been like this even as a young girl. Except for the time he had asked her to dance at her engagement party.

"You've got the smile of an angel," he said, his eyes mesmerizing her. "Makes you look like a little girl. A delectable, saucy little girl," he said as he slowly and expertly began to draw the pins out of her hair.

Pat felt her golden-brown mane come loose. "What are you doing?" she asked, startled, as her hand flew up to stop him. But somehow there was no force in her words or her action. Perhaps something within her was even urging him on.

"Pulling the pins out of your hair," he said softly.

"Don't," she began, the word disappearing.

"Shh," he whispered. "Don't argue with me, Lady Pat," he said, placing the pins on the coffee-table. Deftly, he fanned out her shoulder-length hair, running his strong, sure fingers through it. "There. Now you look like the girl I first met."

"Not unless I have a portrait in the attic, doing my aging for me—and I have no attic," Pat said. She wanted to pull away, but she was caught against the corner of the sofa. She felt the warmth of his nearness coming through to her own body.

"Maybe not, but there's a girl trapped in there, the same bright-eyed girl I met back then," Blaise said seductively. "Patti," he whispered, sending a shiver all through her. "Anyone ever call you Patti?"

"No," she whispered back, riveted to the spot, making no effort to escape now.

"Someone should have called you Patti and pulled the pins out of your hair a long time ago," he said as he turned her face up and kissed her.

In Pat's experience, anticipation had been the best part of everything, because reality had always carried a great deal of disappointment. But now she experienced something quite different. Blaise's kiss was both sweet and sensuous, and rather than satisfying her long-dormant curiosity, it brought an excited rush to her brain, making her pulse race until she could only crave for more. She had thought herself too mature for the sensations that had suddenly burst open like thirsty beings at the first hint of water.

She tried to pull back, but found herself enveloped in his embrace that blocked out the immediate world. She felt his kiss flower in intensity, pulling her out to sea in a craft that she could not control. The room was suddenly unbearably warm as she felt Blaise stroke her cheek tenderly. She had been lonely for so long that she devoured the warmth Blaise offered without realizing what was happening.

The kiss grew, and her remaining thoughts were chased away by shades of red, gold, and dazzling white. The colors swirled about in the inky blackness, forming and reforming glorious rainbows within her.

Engulfed. She was being engulfed. Wait. No, wait. What was she doing? Summoning the great inner strength that had seen her through the past year, Pat gripped Blaise's arms and pushed him away. She blinked, as if calling the world back, beckoning to rational thought.

"I—I don't think you should do that again," she said, rising on legs that felt foreign to her.

"Why?" Blaise asked, watching her for a moment. "Didn't you like it?" He rose, came up behind her, and placed his hands on her shoulders. Pat fought hard to keep from melting back against him. When she gave no answer, he said, "I did."

"Blaise," she began. Blaise. How well he was named. That was what he had kindled within her. A blaze. A blaze unlike any other. No wonder women fell at his feet. Well, she had no time for that. She had a mission, an urgent mission entrusted to her by the man she had spent so much of her life with. She owed Roger her loyalty and a clear head. And if she gave in to this feeling that had suddenly burst upon her, she wouldn't be able to devote herself to her husband's dream. She had to be true to her word.

Blaise waited for her to go on, giving her time, as if he knew she needed to piece herself together. Another man, she felt sure, would have pressed his advantage. She felt her fondness for him grow.

Pat stared at the tiny crack where the drapes did not quite meet. "You do what you do very well, Blaise," she said, choosing her words very carefully. "But I wish you wouldn't practice on me."

"Practice," he repeated, amused, turning her around to face him. "I thought I had it down perfect." His eyes teased her, twinkling and peering into her soul. She found him terribly hard to resist. "I know I didn't offend you, Lady Pat." He said her name almost formally. "You kissed me back, whether you'll admit it to yourself or not."

She felt it best to keep silent for the moment.

"I've been wanting to do that for twenty-one years," he said.

"How could you remember me with all the women in your life?" she asked, trying to be light.

"I remembered," he said, and the seriousness of his tone frightened her for some unknown reason. This was all very melodramatic, she told herself, wanting to step away—but she was riveted to the spot.

"Perhaps you'd better stay at the hotel in town," she found herself suggesting, forcing a steel edge into her voice.

"Where's your famous hospitality? Delia told me you take in stray dogs and cats and feed them."

"You're hardly a stray," she pointed out. Why didn't he withdraw his hands so that she could think clearly?

"Yes, but I'm homeless at the moment nonetheless."

"Can't you stay with Delia?" Pat persisted, searching for a way out.

"She'd want me to be with you," he said simply, his eyes burning into her.

She wanted to meet his gaze head on, the way she did whenever she was under fire, which was quite often these days. But she found herself leery of his power over her. She wondered what Delia could be planning. The older woman knew Blaise's reputation. Was she deliberately throwing them together? Or was Blaise merely telling her that in order to remain at Pat's house?

"All right, stay," Pat said slowly. He moved to kiss her again, but she put her hands against his chest and pushed him away. "But you'll have to behave yourself." This time, she looked him straight in the eye and tried very hard to muster the proper amount of indignation. Who did he think he was, Casanova? It might be a game to him, an interesting pastime, but her affections were not to be toyed with.

"I haven't behaved myself since I was fourteen years old," he said mischievously.

"Then it's time you learned how," she said firmly.

He looked at her, obviously amused by her words and the seriousness of her tone. Playfully, he pushed back the hair that had fallen into her eyes. "Okay, Lady Pat, I'll put on my 'crowned heads of Europe' behavior, but it'll be dull," he warned.

"I'll chance that," she said, wondering if she could let her guard down for a moment as she tried to read the expression on his face.

"Can one old family member kiss another goodnight? After all, what could happen? You're almost forty-one," he teased.

"You've already done that," she replied, arching her brow.

"You're a hard woman, Lady Pat," Blaise said with an indulgent smile.

"I've been told that," she answered, her eyes shining a little. Despite everything, she could not help liking him. Perhaps, she told herself, that was what she was unconsciously afraid of.

He kissed his finger and touched it briefly to her lips. "There, that safe enough, *mon capitan?*" he asked.

"I'll see you in the morning," she said.

"As early as you like," he answered. "You know my room number."

Pat watched him go down the long hallway that led to his room. She realized that Angelica had put him in the room next to hers—or had he put himself there? She waited a few minutes, then picked up her discarded wrap, walked quietly to her bedroom, and closed the door softly behind her.

Tonight, the king-sized bed felt twice as empty as usual as Pat lay in the center of it, propped up with three pillows. On her nightstand was a report about the failure of one of the preliminary tests early last week. Pat thumbed through it, but the words danced meaninglessly in front of her. Instead, she kept seeing Blaise's smile. And each time the image renewed itself, her pulse raced. No doubt about it, Pat thought, he was every bit as overwhelming as he'd always been, and she, sad to say, was not immune to him. Before, there had been Roger, nice, protective, safe Roger. But now the task before her was a poor shield against the charms of a suave world traveler who was, after all, a womanizer. She wondered why Blaise had never married.

She cast the wordy report aside and slid beneath the downy covers. What would her children think if she gave in to the temptation that so clearly existed for her? The thought made her laugh out loud. Usually, such feelings were accompanied with the thought of what one's mother would think, not one's children. By the time you had children to worry about, you had passed the time for smoldering feelings and accelerated heartbeats. At least, she thought, glancing at the wall that separated his room from hers, you should be.

After a while she fell asleep and dreamed of the feel of his lips on hers.

• • •

"Did you enjoy yourself last night?"

Startled, Pat looked up from her desk. Sam had come into her office rather quickly. She felt a blush rise to her face before she could stop it. Sam looked at her curiously—or was it knowingly?

"It was all right," she said offhandedly.

"He really part of Mr. Hamilton's family?" Sam asked.

"He's his cousin," Pat told him, putting down her pen. She smiled. "Hard to believe, isn't it? That the family tree that spawned Jonathan and Allen Hamilton could also come through with Blaise as an offshoot."

"He seemed pretty nice," Sam agreed. "Hope you got some of the rest you need."

Rest? No, she hadn't exactly gotten rest. Her nerves were tuned to a high pitch, as a matter of fact. But it certainly had been a pleasant change from her daily routine. She roused herself from her thoughts and looked at Sam's weathered, impassive face. A hundred years ago, a man like that would have been sitting at a campfire, planning an attack to fend off the white man. Today, she and this stoic, silent person were on the same side. The world was strange, she thought.

"Did you come to quiz me about my 'date,' or is there some other reason for this visit?" she asked with a smile.

Her smile faded as he said, "You've got trouble, boss lady." Sam's tone was always the same, sometimes a bit louder, sometimes a bit quieter, but never expressive of joy or sorrow. She wondered how he managed to keep everything in control.

"What kind of trouble?" she asked, trying to prepare herself for the worst.

"The press is back," he said.

Pat sighed, pushing herself away from her desk as she hunted for her shoes with her bare feet. "Time to pull the wagons in a circle," she said, squaring her shoulders and rising as she slipped on her navy pumps. "No offense," she said, glancing up at him.

"They look like they're out for more than scalps," Sam said, following her to the door.

She turned to look at him, her hand poised on the doorknob. "What are they after now?" she asked.

"Somebody leaked about the component failure."

"And they've come for more pictures of the albatross," she said bitterly. "Any idea who broke the story?"

The incident bothered her greatly. She had come to think of the hundred or so people involved in this project almost as family, certainly a lot closer and more supportive of her than were her actual relatives. To think that one of her employees had turned Judas was almost as difficult as losing the loyalty of Bucky and Sara.

"I'm working on it," Sam said. "Whoever it was, I figure that one of your brothers-in-law has them on the take."

Pat nodded. That made sense. If this project failed, their claim that she was incompetent would be more likely to hold up in court.

Pat walked quickly past Alice, who looked at her nervously. Was it she? Pat wondered. She was privy to all the memos that Pat issued, and the secretary would have seen the report that had been on Pat's nightstand. Alice hadn't been with them all that long, and . . .

No, Pat thought, the young girl was probably just nervous because of all the excitement.

The noise from the workshop was growing as Pat swept down the long steel staircase that led from her office to the ground floor of the plant— the heart of the building, Roger had always called it. At the moment, colorfully dressed representatives of the news media, both T.V. and newspaper, were surrounding Wade Pardy, the head foreman of the project.

When they saw Pat descending the stairs, followed by her faithful companion, Tonto, as the media had christened Sam, they immediately regrouped and encircled her, firing questions and sticking microphones in front of her face. Pat's head began to pound.

"What does this failure mean to the project?"

"Will you be able to finish on time?"

"How about money, Mrs. Hamilton? Story is that there's no more money."

"How are you paying your people?"

"Do you think this was deliberate?"

The last question hit her like a bucket of cold water, sticking out far above the rest. It had been uttered by a bespectacled, thin man who made her think of Allen. He looked as cold-blooded as her brother-in-law, seeming to relish the question he so callously tossed her way.

"No!" she said loudly, although a voice within her would not let the statement go. What if it was true? What if someone was deliberately putting in the wrong components?

"How can you be so sure?" the man pressed, smirking.

"Because I know my people," she snapped.

Sam elbowed the man out of the way, trying to free Pat from the tangle of reporters who were swarming around her, still shouting to get her attention.

"The lady will gladly answer all your questions at the press conference she'll be holding here tomorrow afternoon, ladies and gentlemen. Right now, I'd advise you to leave before the security staff gets nervous."

Pat looked up and saw Blaise coming toward her, parting the crowd with his words as smoothly as Moses parted the Red Sea. Behind him were some guards she had never seen before.

Four

Pat's brows arched as she watched Blaise take control of the situation. He looked like the ideal corporate executive, dressed in his custom-tailored light blue suit, his camel-colored suede coat slung casually over his arms. Perhaps the picture was a little too masterful, Pat thought, feeling unsettled.

"When did you put him in charge, boss lady?" Sam asked, his usually expressionless dark eyes revealing a hint of surprise.

"I didn't," she replied quietly, her face gaining a determined look as the last of the reporters were ushered out the doors. The unfamiliar security guards looked pleased with themselves at the expulsion, as did Blaise, who strode toward Pat. The twenty or so employees looked on, a silent Greek chorus to the minidrama that was unfolding in front of them.

"Any more dragons you want slain?" Blaise asked

lightly as he joined her. He was smiling the easy, radiant smile that made her blood run hot—except that now she was growing increasingly troubled.

"I'm not sure," she said evenly, taking a deep breath. "Who are these people?" She nodded at the two heavyset men who flanked Blaise like bullish, squat bookends protecting a finely bound edition of a beloved classic.

"I thought that in view of your current situation, your security might need beefing up. I was right," he said.

"I see," Pat said, growing angrier. It was an emotion she had not been familiar with before the past year. "I'd like to see you in my office, please," she said, turning around, shoving her hands deep into the pockets of the off-white lab coat she almost always wore at the plant.

Blaise fell into step behind her but managed to be holding the door when she reached the top of the open steel staircase. "After you, Lady Pat," he said, gesturing grandly, his eyes teasing her.

She said nothing until they were back in her office, behind closed doors. Pat was never one for causing scenes—at least, she didn't think so until she heard the harsh sound of her voice. Her mother had always taught her that ladies did not call attention to themselves with sharp, loud words. But ladies of her mother's era were not responsible for getting a dead man's dream into the air.

"What's on your mind?" Blaise asked, perching lightly on the thick arm of the wine-colored leather chair in front of Pat's desk. His deep blue eyes watched her every movement, like a panther about to strike, she thought uneasily.

Pat folded her arms in front of her. "I'm not

sure if I'm better off with the dragon slayer or the dragons," she said tersely.

Blaise paused for a moment, as if considering her words, his eyes never leaving Pat's. "Do I get an English translation, or do I just grow old, trying to puzzle out the mystery behind that statement?"

"Who told you to hire two security men and call a press conference?" she demanded.

Pat was tired of being regarded as a feeble-brained woman, incapable of thinking. Roger's brothers saw her as a fool who had been manipulated into this position and who was hanging on by sheer dumb luck, while her children thought of her as a soft, sentimental idiot chained to a glowing memory of their father. She had fought hard for and earned the respect of the people directly involved in the project, and she was not about to let anyone, even Blaise, try to erode that.

"No one *told* me," Blaise said evenly. "I act by instinct, Lady Pat. I always have. So far, it's served me well. You looked like you needed someone a little more commanding than a man who probably bounced Santa Claus on his knee."

Pat flinched at the remark, thinking of old Steven Ebbs, the current security man. He had been at the plant forever, and she could not bring herself to have him retired or even to wound his pride by hiring younger men. Maybe she wasn't as tough as she tried to be, she thought.

"You might have checked with me," she replied, summoning her composure. "I am, after all, in charge." She watched his eyes for a reaction to her words, but none was evident. He hadn't gotten where he was by wearing his emotions or thoughts broadly on his face, she reminded herself. But she, too, knew something about being a good executive. "This isn't Roger's dream any-more," she said, surprised at how calm the words sounded. "It's *mine*, and I'll fight the devil to hang on to it. Now, I appreciate your help, but if the Eagle is to be a success, we must maintain staff morale and generate as much enthusiasm as possible for this project. I've worked very hard to develop these things, and cannot allow them to be jeopardized by blatant undermining of my author-ity, which is exactly what has happened today. In the future, please check with me before imple-menting any ideas you might have for the manage-ment of Hamilton Enterprises. Is that clear?"

Well, that put him off, said a small voice within her.

Pat watched Blaise's face for signs of erupting anger, but there were none. If he laughed now, she thought, it would be worse, much worse.

But he did neither. Instead, he shook his head, as if he was slightly bemused. "If this is the way you talk to a friend, I'd hate to hear how you talk to an enemy," he said.

His unoffended manner cleared the air and made Pat feel foolish for reacting the way she had. After all, he was merely coming to her rescue the way a gallant knight would have in days of old. Except that Pat no longer believed in the existence of gallant knights.

"Your timing was indeed miraculous. But try to be more careful in the future, okay?" She paused for a moment, then admitted, "Maybe I *did* react a little too strongly."

He took her hand, a gesture warm and reassur-ing, making Pat feel all the more sorry about her harsh words. "Look, I understand what you're going through. It isn't easy being in your position, and you're right, I should have cleared it with you. But to me, the situation looked 'hopeless, but not critical,' " he said with a boyish grin that tugged at Pat's heart. "I jumped the gun. I admit I'm impetuous. That's one of my faults," he confided, his eyes twinkling. "Also one of my virtues." He leaned over and gave her a kiss on the lips, a light, fleeting butterfly kiss that for one magic moment propelled her into another world.

"See? Like that. I just can't help myself," he said with a wink. "Matter of fact . . ."

Before Pat knew it, his strong arms were around her, and his lips were over hers, taking away her badge of leadership and everything else, reducing her to a woman who was experiencing that indefinable thrill of being in a man's arms. She could not believe this was actually happening to her as fingers of warm, glowing fire reached into the center of her being and then radiated out, spreading thin threads of shooting flames. His kiss consumed her tenderly, lovingly, giving only a hint to the fact that beneath it was a growing hunger for her.

Pat's eyes flew open as she roused herself from this other world. She forced herself to return to earth, and Blaise let her go, making no effort to keep her in his arms.

"What was that song when we were younger?" he asked, his eyes possessing her despite his calm outward manner. " 'Kisses Sweeter Than Wine,' " he recalled. "Did anyone ever tell you that?"

"Tell me what?" she stammered, pulling her composure around her like a shield. There were a thousand details to see to, she told herself stern-ly. She had no time to be wooed like an adoles-cent, trembling virgin.

"That you give kisses sweeter than wine," Blaise said, his voice encircling her like a warm sea.

She shook her head. "No."

A smile played on his full, sensuous lips as his eyes swept over her, making her his. And making her very uncomfortable as well. "There're a lot of things people never told you, aren't there?" he murmured, his fingers lightly brushing her cheek.

She pulled back, afraid he would make another advance, afraid of having no resistance to it. "There'll be a lot of things people won't have told me if I don't get back to work," she said, her tone businesslike, or so she hoped. She felt as if she were playacting. Why couldn't she just relax and be herself? she demanded inwardly. No one else made her search for poses to strike in self-defense.

There, that was it. Self-defense. No one else made her feel as if she were totally defenseless, there for the taking. And that wasn't like her at all, she insisted.

Or was it?

"Ever the businesswoman," Blaise said, his tone only slightly teasing. "Lady Pat, I'd love to have you on my team someday," he said. He turned toward the door. "Okay, I'll leave you to your work. But don't overdo it," he warned. "Leave something over for me," he said seductively as he winked and walked out.

Pat clutched at the desk, slowly realizing that her heart was racing and her knuckles were turn-ing white. One moment she saw him as a swash-buckling industrial pirate, ready to sabotage her production plans and zip the Eagle out from under her, and the next moment he was a handsome prince, reducing her knees to water and her brain to mush.

"You're overtired, Patrissa, and this'll never do," she muttered to herself, going over to close the door, which Blaise had left open in his wake.

Pat stopped as she heard the sound of lowered voices. As she looked out, she saw Blaise bending over as he whispered something to Alice, who sat at her desk like a mesmerized puppy.

Pat shook her head as she closed the door. He was probably asking Alice out to lunch in order to wile away an hour or two. Suddenly she stopped in her tracks. What if he was asking Alice questions about the project, questions about what was going into those specification reports? Pat spun around and went back to the door.

But when she cautiously opened it again, Blaise was nowhere to be seen. Alice looked up and blushed. Was that guilt? Pat wondered, closing the door again. She sighed, trying to put all suspicious thoughts out of her mind. She had to stop thinking that everyone was out to undermine the production of the Eagle. Blaise's teasing eyes flashed before her for an instant, but she locked the image away and went out in search of the foreman, Pardy, and Sam.

Pat spent a long day at the office, grabbing a sandwich at her desk for lunch and washing it down with her tenth cup of coffee. She was beginning to think she ran on coffee and stale sandwiches. She did not see Blaise for the remainder of the day.

• • •

Pat sank back into the velour seat of her car, watching old Luis pilot her Mercedes back home, thinking about her brother-in-law. Jonathan was not one to take defeat or humiliation easily. Losing to Pat had been humiliating for him. Pat knew that Jonathan had thought that with his older brother gone, he could assume the mantle of power with Mother Rose's blessings and do what he wanted with Hamilton Enterprises. It was common knowledge that he had intended to sell the factory to a firm that was interested in manufacturing airplanes—solid, dependable, old-fashioned airplanes.

Pat picked up a scrap of paper wedged against the back of the front seat and unconsciously began making a paper airplane. A smile flickered across her lips. Who would have thought that at her age she would still be playing with paper airplanes? She was thinking more of the Eagle than the tiny thing in her hands. She was supposed to be resting and enjoying life now, not struggling against all odds and experiencing— Her thoughts stopped short before they went on to Blaise, which was forbidden territory. She was too tired to think about him.

But yes, yes, she was enjoying life, even if she was dead tired. Enjoying it for the first time in a long, long time. She was about to contribute something important to the world—something absolutely wonderful.

Maybe two something "wonderfuls," a tiny voice suggested before Pat cut it off.

The Mercedes approached the huge black iron

gate of her estate, and Luis, who was one of the two servants Pat had kept after Roger's death, fumbled with the electronic gadget that opened the lock.

"Dios mio," he mumbled into his white stubble of a beard, which never seemed to advance past a five-day growth.

"You have to press harder," Pat reminded him softly.

She heard his dry chortle as he followed her instructions, given for the thousandth time, and the gates sprang open like Olympian guards, clearing a path for the queen.

The car snaked its way up the winding white path, which shone in the moonlight. Every bone in Pat's body cried out for her bed, the ache in her body far outweighing the hungry rumblings in her stomach.

Even climbing the five steps up to the double doors seemed impossible tonight. Three minicrises, with the gnawing information that the money Roger had left was evaporating faster than she had anticipated, had sapped all of Pat's strength. That, and the burning sensation that refused to leave her lips had shot teasingly into her conscious mind at the strangest occasions all through the long day. If she wasn't careful, she admonished herself, she was going to crack up before that Eagle soared.

Pat stood in the doorway, looking down at the three steps that led to the living room with its airy, vaulted ceilings. This house had too many stairs for a one-level house, she thought. Why hadn't she ever noticed that before? Her feet felt like lead as she kicked off her high heels at the door.

Because of the hour, she hadn't expected to find anyone up, except possibly Angelica.

But Angelica was nowhere to be seen. Instead, there in the living room, with his back to her, was Blaise, sitting comfortably on her sofa as if this were his house instead of hers. He could look comfortable anywhere, she supposed, even in hell. Except that he'd never get there, no matter what his deeds. Instead, he'd undoubtedly glibly talk St. Peter into letting him keep the keys to the gates of heaven.

A small smile played on Pat's tired lips as she thought of the little scenario. She saw Blaise glance up in her direction, as if surprised by her sudden appearance. It was then that she noticed he was on the phone. He hung up quickly, and she wondered if he was trying to hide something from her.

She was really getting paranoid, she told herself. The man was into high finance all around the world. Of course he would need to be on the phone sometimes. Pat froze for a moment, too tired to make a decision about Blaise.

His warm smile appeared seductive as he came forward. He wore a sapphire-blue shirt, which was unbuttoned at the top, exposing a chest that would have made a body builder envious. At forty-three he was as trim and taut-muscled as he had been at twenty-one. He had the natural grace that the gods bestowed only on those they loved most, Pat thought absently, noting his pantherlike stride as he crossed the room.

"You look bushed," he said sympathetically, helping her out of her fur coat.

She involuntarily reacted to the feel of his fingers as they brushed against her neck. Tiny pinpricks danced through her as she closed her eyes.

"I am," she said, opening them again, aware that she had sighed rather loudly.

His smile grew even more sensuous. She knew that in a second he would reach for her, and she was not up to that right now. She did not want to open up a font of emotions that could only play havoc with her. There was enough on her mind as it was.

"That's what you get for working overtime," Blaise chided playfully, casually tossing her coat onto a nearby loveseat. His voice was soft and she could almost feel it. Different words would have fit the tone of his voice better, words that spoke of love. . . .

"If the boss doesn't think enough of her project to stay late, how can she expect her people to?" Pat said defensively, and Blaise surprised her by nodding. Or maybe that was just his way of throwing her off balance. She wondered how many women had been disarmed by the light that shone in his blue eyes.

"But any principle carried to the 'nth' degree becomes fanaticism. And you're much too pretty to be a fanatic," he teased, reaching out to touch her face.

Pat stepped back, nearly tripping against the step behind her. Blaise was not slow in catching her in his strong, powerful arms.

"Um, where's Angelica?" Pat asked, seizing the first subject that came to mind as she tried to keep her nerves on an even keel. She wasn't succeeding.

"I sent her to bed," Blaise said. "You're long past needing a duenna," he added, using the Spanish word for chaperon.

"But a Doberman might help," she quipped, and he laughed, his eyes snapping and sparkling. The laugh lines around his mouth deepened, convincing Pat that lines on a man added an endearing quality. It didn't seem fair.

"C'mon," he said, taking her arm gently as he tried to guide her toward the hallway.

"Where?" she asked, digging her heels into the carpet and refusing to budge.

Blaise looked at her upturned face, highly amused. "Give me a little credit, Lady Pat. I'm not about to force you into my bedroom. Dragging a woman by her hair into a man's domain went out a couple of thousand years ago—give or take a hundred," he quipped. "I was only thinking of your welfare. . . . Dinner," he clarified when she gave no response.

She blushed a little, chagrined at her thoughts, then shook her head as if to regain her dignity. "No, thanks, I'm not hungry," she said.

But Blaise would not be put off. "Uh-uh. You need to keep up your strength, and you won't do it by skipping meals." He took her arm again and ushered her off.

"And what do I need to keep my strength up against?" she couldn't help but ask, becoming a trifle giddy in her tired state. "You?"

He clutched his chest dramatically, his dark hair falling into his eyes, looking for all the world like a wayward boy about to pull a prank.

"I? Lady Pat, I'm your ally and friend—and besides, Indian wrestling is not what I have in mind when the time comes," he whispered confidentially, looking her up and down with a promise that she could not help but recognize.

"What do you mean, 'when the time comes'?" Pat demanded, now fully alert. "You sound very sure of yourself."

Blaise smiled for a moment, which made it all the worse. Then he replied, "I was taught to play poker by the best—and he said never put all your cards on the table unless you're sure you have a winning hand."

She did not know what to make of that. She realized that he was leading her past the dining room. "Wait," she protested, but Blaise ignored the long, darkened room and purposefully led her on. "I thought you said we were eating."

"I did."

'Well, you just went past the dining room," she said suspiciously, knowing that they were going in the direction of his room.

Blaise shook his head. "These formal dining rooms are designed by frigid women and effeminate men who are trying to retain population zero. You could *bowl* on that table," he said. "I've seen enemy camps in the Far East set their tents up closer than the opposite ends of it."

"We used it for entertaining," she said defensively, thinking of her cherry wood dining-room set.

"Nothing very entertaining about having to shout to be heard," Blaise told her, entering the warmly lit kitchen. It was bathed in candlelight. "Your dinner, Lady Pat," he said with a flourish of his hand, which indicated the little kitchen table, "is waiting in the cozy breakfast nook, where, if I position myself just right, our knees will touch." A teasing smile was on his lips.

Pat didn't know whether to laugh or cry as he settled her into the far side of the nook. And Blaise was right. The warmth of the kitchen was infinitely preferable to the alienating, formal dining room. He seemed instinctively to know everything, she thought as he removed her dinner from the warming tray and placed it before her.

Suddenly she wondered if he knew how very lonely she had been. Looking up into his warm, liquid blue eyes as he sat down next to her, Pat was sure that he did.

Five

"Have you thought about what you're going to say at your press conference tomorrow?" Blaise asked Pat, patiently repeating his question.

Pat blinked, as if coming out of a daze. For a moment his eyes had held her captive. They had made her think of wonderful, impossible things that she knew could never be. But his words brought her back to the present, with all its responsibilities.

"You mean *your* press conference, don't you?" Pat asked wryly. "You were the one who called it."

"Don't split hairs," Blaise said, pouring her a glass of wine, which shimmered in the light of the flickering candle. It felt so terribly intimate, being here like this with him, and Pat was grateful that he was talking about the jet instead of trying to woo her. She needed a clear, uncluttered mind

now more than ever. "You need that press conference," he told her matter-of-factly.

"Oh? And why, pray tell?" she asked, taking a
sip of the wine, which wound its warm way
through her entire body, relaxing her instantly.

Blaise leaned back slightly. "You're a babe in
the woods, Lady Pat. It's always good to have the
power of the press on your side. Make them think
they're your friends, and if they don't have to bust
their tails for your story, they'll usually treat you
with kindness. The Eagle wouldn't be such an
albatross if you had called a conference sooner,"
he said.

"I don't believe in baring my soul," Pat said.

Blaise's smile encompassed more than their conversation about the press. "There's a lot to be said
for 'baring' things at the right time." His eyes
lingered on her for a moment. "This is the right
time to cooperate with the press. If you wait any
longer, they'll become an obstacle for you. Tell
them everything."

She raised her eyebrow archly, putting down
her fork. "Tell them that we're on the verge of
going broke?"

He shook his head. "No, not that honest. Listen, I'll help you get through this," he promised.
"That is, provided I'm allowed."

Pat shifted uncomfortably. What if he was really
working for Jonathan and Allan or some other
outside party? She wasn't ready to trust him completely. Some of Blaise's battles for control might
have been won in the bedroom, but she was not
about to let the Hamilton jet become a casualty
just because she had a queasy feeling in the pit of
her stomach.

Blaise looked a trifle annoyed at her hesitation. "It's going to be awfully hard helping you, Lady Pat, if I have to wait each time until 'Simon Says' I can take two giant steps forward. I'm used to leaping—"

"I bet you are." The words slipped out before she had a chance to stop them.

He laughed. "You know, Patti," he said, and the name catapulted her back into a world that had never really existed for her, "I'd like to sweep you into my arms and carry you upstairs to your bedroom like Clark Gable in *Gone with the Wind*. You deserve that sort of treatment. But you don't have any stairs," he said mournfully, his eyes already making love to her.

"You could try walking up and down the steps in the living room a few times," she said dryly.

"No, not the same thing," he said sadly, then suddenly came around and picked her up easily in his arms. Pat was too startled for words as he began to carry her down the hall and past Angelica's room toward his own.

"Well, so much for foreplay," he said with a twinkle in his eye.

"And during-play and after-play," she said firmly, not knowing whether he was kidding, and terribly afraid to take the chance of finding out. "Put me down, Blaise," she ordered.

"Why?" he asked, but did as she asked. "We're both consenting adults."

"You're consenting," she pointed out, her heart pounding. "I'm not."

He ran his finger along her lower lip. An involuntary tremor threatened to break loose. Pat maintained control, though she yearned for the promised excitement that lay just beyond his bedroom door.

"You don't even know what I want you to consent to," he teased.

"Oh, I've a pretty good idea," she answered, amusement coming into her voice. He was so adorable, despite everything she thought he was trying to do. If only . . . "And I'm past that," she said firmly, more to herself than to him.

Solemnly, Blaise studied her, then took her pulse. Pat stared at him, puzzled.

"Pulse okay," he said, letting go of her wrist, then peering into her eyes. "All vital signs seem to be there," he observed. "When did you die?" he asked mildly.

"I didn't die!" she cried.

He loomed over her, tall and broad-shouldered, standing bigger than life and filling all the space in her small hallway. "Then you're not past 'that,'" he said, bending his head and kissing her softly.

The kiss lasted forever, intensifying until there was nothing left but infinite, all-consuming passion. She was drowning—drowning in a yearning that was more fervent than anything she had ever known. She had fully believed that after years of unfulfillment, the desire within her that had been born in the days when she had believed in romance was dead. But it wasn't. It was alive and well and in full splendor—but she couldn't allow it to be used against her, and she wasn't sure if she was just a passing fancy for Blaise, or if he viewed her as the Hamilton Factory.

Get out now, *now*, before you've gone under, something pleaded within Pat, something that had always been her lifeline to the world. With her heart beating fast in her ears, she pushed Blaise back, wedging her small, delicate hands against the overwhelming heat that came from his hard chest.

"Blaise, please, no," Pat said, trying with all her might to keep her voice from shaking.

Blaise cocked his head slightly, still keeping her in his arms. "You certainly are something, Lady Pat," he said softly. "I'm used to hearing 'Blaise, please, yes.'" There was something serious, something almost—sad—in his eyes.

Yes, yes, she meant the world to him, Pat told herself sarcastically, and her refusal would cause him to run off to a monastery in Tibet and become celibate. Think, Patrissa, think, she chided herself.

"But, as you wish," Blaise said, releasing her.

Sadly, Pat felt the strong pressure of his arms fade. Would it have been so wrong to give in . . . ?

"I'm sure you'll recover," Pat said, trying to sound light.

"I won't cover that bet," he said quietly, then a smile played on his lips for a moment. "I have the rest of forever, Lady Pat," he said, fondly touching her honey-colored hair, which was so neatly arranged. He pulled out a pin mischievously and handed it to her. "I can wait."

As if he'd wait for any woman, Pat thought as she got ready for bed, acutely aware that he was in the other room. Her body was more aware than she cared to admit, and she vainly tried to think of other things. Blaise Hamilton was a charming womanizer, she told herself firmly, then relented.

No, that wasn't quite fair. He didn't use women. He enjoyed them, giving them a wonderful time while he was there. No strings. No promises. She climbed into bed and told herself that all this contemplation was fruitless. Besides, she needed her rest. Tomorrow was not that far away.

The press conference went better than she had thought it would. Pat had worked with Blaise all morning, preparing to answer the questions that would most likely be asked. Even so, she went into it with icy hands, keeping her head high as she stepped past an ocean of people armed with pens and papers and cameras, ready to take down every word. The conference, called for three, was held in what had recently been dubbed "the problem room," where the "bugs" that plagued the Hamilton jet's progress were ironed out. Pat was used to seeing engineers standing about there, chewing pencils and speaking a language that had once been foreign to her. The room, with its long oak table and the afternoon light streaming in from a wall of windows on one side, had seemed almost like a second home to her. Now it was the site of the enemy camp.

Blaise squeezed her hand as she sat down, as if sensing her thoughts. He took the seat next to her, a place she would normally have given to the foreman, Wade Pardy, who now stood off to the side and scowled. Pat looked to her left at Sam's profile. Good old Sam, she thought, having him around was such a comfort at a time like this.

"I think we can start now," Blaise whispered to

Pat as he leaned forward, covering the microphone in front of her.

The smell of his cologne invaded her senses. What an odd thing to think of at a time like this, she told herself. Suddenly the low-keyed noise around her became an organized din as the warriors of the press took aim with their pens and tape-recorders, waiting for her to give the first words. A naturally shy person, Pat wondered how she had come to be in this situation. Well, here goes nothing, she thought.

She raised her head high and forced herself to look out at the sea of faces, trying to turn them into people rather than a mass of swarming vultures.

"Ladies and gentlemen of the press," she said with a throat that was dry, "I'm very glad you came, giving me this opportunity to fully inform you about my husband's—about our project. I hope to clear up any 'mysteries' or misconceptions that you might have." She looked around at the wide show of eager hands before her and picked one out, fervently hoping that the question would be an easy one.

The hand belonged to a hard-looking reporter who quickly went to the heart of the matter. "The Hamilton jet has been called everything from a paper plane to the new *Spruce Goose*," he said, referring to Howard Hughes's grounded plane. "Just exactly what is it?" he asked, his tone a trifle more subdued now beneath Pat's unwavering gaze. Pat could command respect when she tried, having the manner of a cool, refined lady, hence Blaise's nickname for her. It was only Roger's family who insisted on treating her in a high-handed, demeaning manner.

"The Hamilton jet is designed to be a business aircraft that, upon completion, will fly at nearly the speed of a jet, using only one-third to one-quarter of the fuel," she said.

A buzz went up in response to her remark. The next question was about how this could be possible. Was there a magician in the fuselage or in the jet engines, or was the plane really made of paper as rumored?

"No," Pat said with a smile, "cloth." She looked around at the bewildered and bemused faces. "To make the terminology simple for you, the plane's outer shell is made of cloth and glue."

"How about making the terminology complicated?" someone shouted from the background without waiting to be called on. Obviously there was doubt as to the truth of Pat's statement.

"Okay," she said gamely, "the entire structure is to be made of an advanced carbon fiber and epoxy composite. This cloth," she said, nodding at an employee who stood waiting off to the side; he came forward, carrying a sample of the material she was talking about, "is half the weight of aluminum." She saw the skepticism in the eyes of some of the people closest to her. "And twice as strong," she concluded firmly.

Pat motioned for the young employee to pass the cloth along the first row, which he did. The cloth was gingerly touched and poked in disbelief.

"And this'll fly?" someone else wondered out loud as he had his turn at feeling the material.

"This'll fly," Pat replied with conviction.

A woman had the floor next and she rose in

front of Pat, looking like the epitome of the "new woman." It was obvious that she was more interested in Pat's role in the project than in the project itself. "Two years ago, you were a 'homemaker,' and now you're the chairman of the board of a hundred-million-dollar business. Does this situation frighten you?" she asked.

"When progress is involved," Pat said carefully, "you have no time to give vent to or even to think of personal feelings," she said, glancing unconsciously at Blaise. Think of your own words, Patrissa, she warned. "My personal fears, whatever they might be, cannot stand in the way of finishing this project."

"Won't your plane jeopardize a lot of other small-plane manufacturers?" another man challenged. "How do you feel about putting them out of business?" he pushed harshly.

"About the same way the advocates of the Industrial Revolution felt, I suppose," she said tersely, refusing to back down. She noted a look of admiration from a few of the people. "There'll be new jobs available, *different* jobs, manufacturing planes just as good as this one. Better, someday," she said proudly.

The man sat down, put well into his place.

Pat felt Blaise's approval as his eyes cheered her on and an excitement surged through her.

Questions of a more technical nature were then asked, just before someone brought up the subject of money and funding. Pat licked her lips, about to answer that they were hoping for backing—begging was more like it, she thought. But suddenly she felt Blaise stirring next to her. She looked at him.

"I'd like to answer that," Blaise began, then looked at Pat. "May I?" he asked, and she knew he was having fun with her, recalling last night's conversation about "Simon Says."

"Yes," Pat replied, keeping a straight face as she nodded. What was he going to say? she wondered. She was totally unprepared for his statement.

Blaise shifted in his seat and immediately the room was his without a word. Pat marveled at his command.

"For those of you who don't know me," he said, his eyes warmly encircling the crowd, turning it into a social group, "I'm Blaise Hamilton, Mrs. Hamilton's cousin-in-law. I've recently been appointed special financial adviser to Hamilton Enterprises."

Pat tried to hide her surprise at his words, but she was sure Blaise saw the fire that appeared in her eyes.

"And funding for the project is generously coming in from several sources. One, of course, is the Hamilton Corporation itself. Roger Hamilton provided quite handsomely for his newest 'baby.' We are also getting large sums from advance orders. And presently we are about to close negotiations with another government that is willing to advance us thirty million dollars in exchange for having a Hamilton jet factory built there."

"What government?" a reporter asked.

Blaise raised his hands in a quieting gesture. "Entirely friendly, I assure you. But at the moment, negotiations are delicate, and until they are finalized, details have to be kept confidential. Sorry. You'll be the first to know when everything is settled," he promised with his charismatic smile, and for some reason, that was that.

The rest of the press conference passed quickly, and soon Pat was watching the men and women file out, with several of the reporters still hovering around Blaise. Mainly women, she noted, gathering up her notes from the table and slowly, deliberately, putting them in order.

Sam rose quietly. "What country?" he asked as soon as there was no one near them.

"News to me," Pat admitted, a grimace playing at the corners of her mouth as she watched Blaise talking easily to the circle of people around him.

Sam shook his head. "I don't know about him, boss lady."

"Neither do I, Sam, neither do I," she said with a sigh. "Sam, could you—"

"I'm already gone," the Indian said, second-guessing her and starting to clear the room of the other employees who had been present.

Pat caught Pardy grumbling to someone about being kept in the dark and not being trusted. She found the tall Indian again and whispered, "Explain to him that I'm as much in the dark as he is." She knew Sam didn't like the task, because he and Pardy did not get along, but she also knew that Sam would do anything she told him to, for which she was grateful.

Pat turned her attention back to Blaise. There were only two reporters left now, one of whom was the "new woman," who was very obviously taken with Blaise. Pat began to wonder if any woman was truly immune to him.

She hung back, waiting, feeling like a schoolgirl who had to wait her turn with the handsome professor. Finally, everyone was gone and Pat and Blaise stood in the empty room.

Blaise turned, sensing her presence. She was surprised that he even knew she had stayed behind, considering the attention he had gotten from the other women. But he was not one to be drunk on his own prowess. Business was first, always first, with someone like him.

"I think it went very well, Lady Pat. You handled yourself like a champion. I'm proud of you."

His words of praise almost made her forget her anger at not having been informed. But she managed to pull some of her fire back into her eyes. "What country?" she asked.

"Hmm?" he asked mildly as he handed her neatly stacked notes to her.

"What country is funding us?" she asked more clearly, her tone a little more demanding.

"Oh. I don't know yet," he replied truthfully, the admission not troubling him in the slightest.

It did Pat. "What!" she cried.

"Easy, Lady Pat," he said soothingly. "Some country will come through. As a matter of fact, with that little item mentioned in the articles, we're sure to get several offers hoping to counter the 'offer' we already have."

"But what if we don't?" she demanded.

He looked at her patiently, and said slowly, as if to a child in need of educating, "You have to think positively, Lady Pat. If you don't believe you'll win, there's no reason to get into the game."

"This isn't a game, Blaise. This is very, very important to me and I won't have you treating it as if it's an afternoon's diversion!" she said hotly.

"This may be small potatoes to you, but it's not to me."

Blaise seemed unaffected by her tirade. "Did you see the way those reporters looked when they left the room?" he asked mildly. "They were impressed, Lady Pat."

Pat beckoned to the part of her that was the successful manager, and was able to respond to him softly but assertively. "I acknowledge your glowing background in high finance and accept the possibility that you had sound reasons for saying what you did. But if you're going to help me, which was your idea in the first place, you've got to keep certain things in mind. How do you think I felt when you announced a financial agreement of which I was unaware? Certain members of my staff now believe that I have been withholding information from them. I just can't have you ruining the atmosphere of cooperation and trust that has kept this project moving so far."

A flicker of regret passed over Blaise's otherwise stoic expression, and he put his hands on her shoulders. "I must confess that you've got a point. In all honesty, the idea of a foreign investor never occurred to me until I started speaking. But you've got to admit that it was a brilliant move. With another government coming into the picture, we've taken the Eagle out of the realm of 'small potatoes,' as you call it, and made it an international project. Something your staff is going to be proud of working for—not just their shares or their memory of Roger. Now they're working on something that is seriously going to be looked at as a piece of history. Is that so bad?" he asked.

Pat considered his words carefully, and his

boyish enthusiasm won her over. "I never doubted your instincts, Blaise," she said with an indulgent smile. "I suppose you're right on that count."

He took his hands from her shoulders. "Of course I am," he told her, grinning. "It's my business to be right—about everything," he said with a wicked wink, making Pat think fleetingly of his prophecy last night that she would be his.

"But what if no country comes forward!" she persisted.

"About everything," he repeated, then kissed her and walked away.

The room echoed his voice and his presence long after he was gone. Pat walked to the wall of windows and looked down at the parking lot two stories below. She saw Blaise get into his car and speed away. Was this her knight in shining armor at long last? Or was she going to be bitterly disappointed? With her mind in turmoil, she walked out of the conference room.

When Pat got home that night, Blaise was not around. Angelica informed her that he was "out," which was the only message he had left. He was "out" the following night as well. And the following. Pat did not see him for four days and began to believe that he had either decided to leave or was avoiding her. In either case, she had too much to do to be concerned about his presence, or the lack of it.

But she was.

And then, almost a week later, she was awakened by someone knocking on her bedroom door. She glanced at the luminous dial on her clock and saw that it was just a little past midnight. Was it Angelica? she wondered, switching on the light and finding her way to the door quickly, entirely forgetting her robe.

But as she opened the door, she found Blaise standing there, an excited light in his eyes. A different sort of light came into them for a moment as the words on his lips hung suspended while he looked at her appreciatively.

The lavender nightgown she wore was sleeveless, its lace design coming up around her breasts, which were ripe and full and still proudly high. The lacy material hugged them, adding to the desirable air about her as the folds of nightgown fell gently to the ground.

"The prodigal son has returned with good news," he said flippantly, his eyes never leaving her body.

Pat suddenly realized that she was not wearing her robe and that, illuminated by lamplight, her nightgown was fairly see-through. She swallowed to take the dryness out of her throat. "Just a second," she said, turning around to pick up her robe.

But when she turned back, Blaise was in the room and the door was shut behind him. Pat's nerve endings tingled, sounding an alarm. She tried to remind herself that she had always been able to laugh off advances when they had come from other men, both before and after Roger's death. But there was no laughter now as an excitement fought to take hold of her.

"Did you miss me?" he asked in a sultry, husky voice.

"Well, I did wonder where you were," she admitted, trying to sound disinterested. "Most of my houseguests don't just disappear into thin air without leaving some kind of word behind," she said, walking away from him.

"I left word," he said, coming closer to her, almost stalking her, Pat thought desperately.

" 'Out' is only one word. Usually I get at least a whole sentence," she said dryly.

"Next time I'll leave a postcard in twenty-five words or less," he promised. " 'Dear Lady Pat, I'm out, tilting your windmills.' How's that?"

"What?" she asked, shaking her head. His statement made no sense to her. Neither did the growing longing she was feeling. She was getting increasingly nervous over the realization that she wanted him—had always wanted him.

Blaise reached for her hand and pulled her closer to him.

Six

Blaise's long, sweeping fingers slid up and down Pat's body, pulling her against him as he once more captured her lips, draining words of reproach from her and pulling forth the sweetness that had never before been allowed to blossom. Pat felt engulfed and overpowered by him, and the determination to keep business uppermost in her mind died a sharp, quick death as the hungry woman within her opened up to him.

Pat thought she was on fire as his hands explored the softness that was hidden by the gauze-like nightgown, which comprised the flimsy barrier between them. Somehow, it was no longer on her shoulders, held up only by the force of his body pressing against hers. As Blaise allowed a tiny space between them, the lavender material loosened from its final perch on her nipples and floated to her waist as its place was taken by his cupped hands, which rubbed a sea of molten lava over Pat with each caress.

His lips were everywhere, kissing her neck, the hollow of her throat, the delicate points of her shoulders, tenderly yet hungrily devouring her as she felt herself pulled closer and closer to him. How long had it been since she was desired, truly desired, by a man? Roger's lovemaking in total had never even approached this plateau. It had been tender, but awkward at times, and far from satisfying. She had believed that that was all there was—until Blaise.

Drunkenly, Pat made a stab at control. "Whe—where have you been?" she asked.

"Then you did miss me," he said against her ear, his hot breath making her pulse throb erratically and her body plead to be his.

But Pat had thought with her mind, not her emotions, for so long that there was still a thread of resolve left to cling to. And she did.

She stepped back. "Blaise, I don't know what you're trying to do—"

He stopped, then smiled that engaging grin of his, his eyes sensual. "I thought I was making it pretty clear. Just let me go on showing you," he urged, coming toward her again. "You'll catch on soon enough."

Pat put up her hands, making a barrier in front of her. "I don't want to 'catch on,' " she lied. "I want to produce the Hamilton jet."

"In here?" he asked, looking around the blue and mocha room. "How small are the businessmen using this jet supposed to be?"

"Stop laughing at me," she ordered with a pleading note in her voice. "I'm serious."

She slipped the nightgown back up, hiding her nakedness from his sight while he gazed at her unabashedly. She could feel the blush going up to the roots of her hair. Blaise had a habit of bringing springtime back into her life, a time when her innocence was still intact and the world was a lot lighter and gayer.

"So am I," he said under his breath. "Yes," he said aloud, taking her hands in his, but this time it was a comforting gesture of friendship. "I know you are." He gazed at her for a moment, as if shifting his thoughts around.

"Which is why," he continued, his eyes kind, "you're going to have a party."

"A party?" she echoed in surprise. "What is it that I'm supposed to be celebrating?" she asked, wondering what he was up to now.

"Hopefully, money," he said dryly.

"Does this riddle have an answer?" she asked, her heart still throbbing violently.

"You are going to be entertaining the about-to-be investors in Roger's brainchild," Blaise said, sitting down on her lounge chair in the corner of the room.

"Shouldn't I meet them in a board meeting?" she asked, careful not to sit near Blaise.

"All in good time, Lady Pat. First, we see them through a wineglass and make nice to them. Friendly people can be touched for money much more easily than unfriendly people," he said.

"But I haven't time for a party," she protested, rising from the edge of her bed and standing in front of him.

"Have you time for bankruptcy?" he asked evenly, looking up at her.

She cast her eyes down, staring at the carpet. "No."

"Then you have time for a party. Tomorrow night," he said. "The invitations are already out," he added.

She looked at him in surprise. "How did you—?"

"Never ask me how. I have my ways, Lady Pat," he said, lacing his fingers together and resting his head against them as he watched her. "You shouldn't wear things like that. A gunnysack would be far better," he said, "if you want to be left alone."

"I don't usually have parades coming through my room," she said evenly.

"Lucky thing," he replied as he rose and went to the door. "You rained on mine." He stopped in the doorway. "Oh, by the way, I think I have a country for you."

Her eyes grew wide as she fairly bounced across the room to the door, putting her hand on his to stop his exit. "Wait a minute!" she cried. "What country? Explain!"

But the look on Blaise's face was mischievous. "I'm tired. I just flew back," he said mysteriously. "And all this resistance has sapped my strength," he said, stretching before her. The movement was slow, purposeful, and utterly sensual. "We'll talk in the morning," he said, and left.

Pat slammed the door behind him in frustration. She heard him laugh softly as the door to his own room closed.

This had to be a ploy to get her to come to him, she thought. At times, his ruthless teasing was too exasperating to bear.

●   ●   ●

Angelica came through like a trooper the next evening.

When Pat came home from the plant at three-thirty, she found that Blaise had called in a maid service and had placed three young girls under Angelica's direction, telling her just what he wanted done. Normally, Angelica did not like having anyone dictate her movements, but Pat noted that she acquiesced to Blaise's requests easily enough. The house was suitably decorated for the occasion, and food was being brought in from a restaurant that specialized in exotic dishes.

"Houston Fields is a gourmet," Blaise explained to Pat as she looked questioningly at him when the caterer hurried past her into the kitchen. She grasped his arm in time to keep from being trampled by two men carrying in trays of hors d'oeuvres.

Blaise did not seem to mind in the slightest as he smiled down at Pat while one of the maids looked on enviously. "Not now, Lady Pat," he said playfully.

She shot him an annoyed look, and the maid quickly hurried out of the living room.

"Well, at least I know the name of one of my guests," she said flippantly.

"I'll fill you in on the others while I help you dress for dinner," Blaise offered, about to follow her out of the room.

Pat turned, standing her ground firmly. "I've been getting myself dressed ever since I was in the first grade," she said.

"And hasn't it been lonely?" he asked devilishly.

"Blaise Hamilton," Pat said, half-amused and

half-desperate, "you are the most impossible man I have ever run into!"

"Good," he said, coming after her. "Now shall we go?" he asked, taking her elbow.

"I go," she said in slow, deliberate fashion. "You stay," she said, pointing to his chest.

Blaise snapped his fingers. "Foiled again. Okay, then take a bubble bath."

"A what?"

"You know, that luxurious thing movie stars are always doing," he prompted.

She cocked her head. "Why?" she asked suspiciously.

"To make you feel sexier," he replied, a smile playing on his lips.

"It's the jet we want to fly, not me," she responded dryly.

"You fly what you want," Blaise said, his eyes caressing her, "and I'll fly what I want. Besides, Fields likes his women feminine."

"I'm not anyone's woman," she said archly.

"Yes you are," he said softly.

She threw up her hands and walked out.

"The bubble bath is on the sink in your bathroom," Blaise called after her, stepping out of the way of a delivery man. "Half an hour should do it."

"So now you're an expert on bubble baths," she said with a mocking tone as she turned back to look at him.

The look on Blaise's face was positively wicked. "I've shared a lot," he said.

Pat turned away without another word.

She had no intention of taking a bubble bath, meaning to shower quickly and be ready. But

Blaise and Angelica seemed to have everything under control, so, half out of boredom, half out of a desire to recapture a time when she was free to take long bubble baths, she poured the pink crystals into the sunken Grecian tub and watched the suds seductively rise up to her touch.

Tying her sunlight-brown hair up on top of her head with a ribbon, Pat gingerly slid into the steaming hot water, letting it erode the tense, tired ache from her body. Slowly, ever so slowly, she relaxed and let the bath work its magic. She closed her eyes and allowed herself to let go completely for the first time since Roger's death. Blaise did have something here, she admitted grudgingly.

It was only after she had opened her eyes and returned to the present that she realized the noise that had roused her was the soft turning of her bathroom doorknob. She smiled in satisfaction, having locked the door before she had gotten into the tub.

"It's locked," she called out triumphantly.

"Playing hard-to-get only makes the sport more interesting," Blaise said with a laugh. "Enjoying yourself?"

"Yes," she replied.

"Good. Knew you would. Sure you don't want your back scrubbed?" he offered, his voice sexy.

"No!"

"How about your front?"

Someone like Blaise was not above picking locks! "Blaise, if you don't leave this instant, I'll scream!"

"No, that only happens *during* . . . not before," he said seductively, then paused. "Okay, I'll retreat." She heard him go—she thought.

It was a long time before Pat left the luxury of

the tub. By then, the water was cold and had lost its magic. She got out and quickly toweled herself dry, then put on her bathrobe, leaving the shelter of the bathroom carefully. She looked behind her door, expecting Blaise to pop out.

When he didn't, she felt a little foolish, but told herself that her actions were justified. Blaise was totally unpredictable.

As she made her way through the bedroom, a question that had been raised at the press conference came to mind. A reporter had wanted to know about competition between Hamilton and other manufacturers of small passenger planes. It wasn't so farfetched an idea that one of them could be behind Blaise's sudden appearance. Curtailing or completely sabotaging the Eagle's production would benefit a lot of people in the short range, she thought angrily, becoming that much more determined to withstand Blaise's attentions. She felt it wise not to ignore the possibility of his covert deceitfulness.

She dressed carefully, wanting to create a good appearance at the party. If these were truly investors who were popping up on her doorstep— and where had Blaise found them when all her pleadings had yielded polite "maybes" at best?— when she wanted her chance at them, no matter what Blaise really had in mind. She chose a shimmering silver-blue floor-length dress with long, straight sleeves and one suggestive slit that traveled practically the length of her left leg. The neckline was deeply cut in the back, showing off her fine, sculptured shoulder blades, and had a slight V neck in the front. She brushed her hair down and then back, adding height to her appearance.

"Very nice," Blaise said when she joined him in the living room. He was issuing last-minute orders to the three maids while Angelica was busy in the kitchen, setting things up undoubtedly to please herself.

"Thank you," Pat murmured, pleased at his simple words.

"The dress is nice too," he added, a wicked twinkle dancing in his eyes.

Pat laughed, looking at him fondly for a moment. "I don't remember, were you always this glibly charming and free with your compliments?"

"Yes and no," he said. She thought he looked particularly handsome, silhouetted by the light from the white stone fireplace. The few dimly lit lamps added to the intimate mood. She tried to concentrate on his words and not the effect he was having on her. "I was always charming. The nurse told my mother I was the most charming baby in the nursery," he said, his full lips given to a smile.

"You probably made a pass at her," she said, trying to lapse into light cheerfulness.

"But," he continued, ignoring her comment. "I am not always free with my compliments. I bestow them only when they're appropriate—and you are a vision," he said, holding out her hands as if to drink in the full picture she made.

Pat refused to take his words seriously. "That line might have worked twenty years ago, but I know better now. The tragedy of life is that men grow better-looking as they grow older and women just grow older," she said with a sigh.

"Need I remind you yet again of that commercial about getting better?"

"That's just to sell a product," she said, tossing the comment aside.

"You, Lady Pat, could sell any product you wanted," he said, and the way he said it, she could almost believe him. "Some people," he said, and she realized that he still had her hands and was not letting go, "like their women older."

"Boy scout instincts, no doubt."

"No one could ever accuse me of being a boy scout," he said, and Pat had to smile. "And there is something fascinating about a woman who has seen a little of life. She has maturity and experience and is not a mere giggling ingenue," he said seriously. "At twenty, there's just the rosebud, the blush on the bloom that is to come. At your age, the promise that was is just beginning to be fulfilled," he said, his eyes tender with a hint of something that she could not quite believe.

He took her into his arms, and this time the idea of resistance was far from Pat's mind. His eyes sparkled as his lips brushed gently against hers, as if he was taking care not to smudge her lipstick.

"How come they haven't made you emperor of the world yet?" she murmured, trying to deny her "ingenuelike" racing pulse.

"I'm working on it," he replied, his voice enticing and low against her ear.

But the doorbell rang and terminated what might have come to pass. Blaise released her, suddenly becoming the worldwide financier about to entertain prospective investors.

Reluctantly, she gave up the lover who had been

next to her only a moment before and joined Blaise at the door to greet her guests.

Houston Fields was a tall, wide man with a gusto for living and an even greater one for eating. He arrived with an entourage of men who were his business associates and friends, one condition depending upon the other. They brought their wives. Everyone in the party seemed to know Blaise.

Pat wondered if there was anyone whom Blaise did not know, as he led her through the introductions. Houston's wife, Eloisa, was a Eurasian with lovely, slanted eyes and a quiet, regal bearing that could easily have belonged to a princess. She and the women kept discreetly quiet while male voices were raised in friendly comaraderie. They sipped wine politely and partook of the hors d'oeuvres while a five-piece orchestra, bathed in the light from the glowing fireplace, provided soft, dreamy music.

Dinner was a success and all appeared to be going smoothly.

Houston Fields was the center of attention, a position he was used to by virtue of his girth, his millions, and his booming voice. He had, to Pat's relief, an amazing sense of humor. The first time he slapped his knee in merriment, Pat thought he was going to knock over the table. It was barely steadied in time.

Eventually, over after-dinner drinks and dessert, the matter of the Eagle was brought up. Houston cast a round, tiny eye at Pat, as if studying her critically.

"So this paper bird of yours can really fly?" he asked, his voice suddenly serious. Business had a way of sobering everything, Pat thought as she nodded.

"Yes. We have some of the finest engineers in the industry working at the plant," she said, warming to her subject. "It'll not only fly, but it'll revolutionize air travel as we know it. There's no telling what possibilities lie ahead," she said with enthusiasm.

"Yes, well . . ." Houston cleared his throat, and Pat thought she was losing him.

Quickly, she began to tell him about the plane's inception, how her husband had seen every detail through, spending countless nights up with the plans. While it was true that he had employed the finest engineers, there was no doubt that it had been his brainchild all the way. He had been the inspiration behind it—and he had been the creator of more than one successful invention, although none as revolutionary and seemingly as impossible as the Eagle.

Pat recited the plane's specifications, knowing them better now than she knew her own name, and she could see that she was impressing Houston ever so slightly, although he kept a "damn poker face" on, just the way Blaise had said all good financiers did.

When she was finished, Pat watched Houston lean back expansively, still watching her face. "Well, little lady, you can join my organization as a salesman, er, woman," he corrected with a laugh for her benefit, "any day. Of course, it's a little unfair of me to make you go through the paces, since Blaise here handed me everything I could ever possibly want to read on the subject before I got

here. But it was nice finding out just how much
you really believe in this plane of yours."

Through her paces? her mind echoed. Like a
trained horse? But her anger simmered down after
a moment. The big man had meant it as a compliment, undoubtedly. Pat had not traveled in her
husband's circle of friends for twenty years without learning how to read a person's nature, so she
kept her peace and smiled.

"Does that mean we have a pledge from you?"
she asked, hoping that she sounded sufficiently
subdued. She had been through so many disappointments, and even Roger's friends had turned
their backs on the project now that he was gone.

"That it does, little lady, that it does. The meal
here alone was worth a goodly sum," Houston
said happily, patting his ample bulk.

Pat glanced at Blaise and saw him nod and
smile at her. A feeling of relief mingled with joy
and possibly even foolish love washed over her as
Blaise, who sat at the opposite end of the dining-
room table, gave her the high sign. He rose and
walked toward her. Her eyes slid appreciatively
over the fine figure that he cut. His navy jacket
was buttoned, accenting the impressive difference
between his waist and his shoulders, and Pat was
not unaware that several of the wives looked at
her with envy, imagining, no doubt, that there
was something going on between her and Blaise.
She put the thought aside.

"If Houston is finished, I'd like to adjourn to the
living room, where we can all gather in a little
closer," Blaise said, helping Pat out of her chair.

A warm thrill passed through her as his hand
touched her bare shoulder. He had done it. She

had misjudged the man. Blaise had succeeded where she had failed in rounding up financing. Surely she could stop distrusting him now.

The relief made her heart sing.

Fields and his party stayed until well after eleven, then left after promising a million dollars.

"I can't believe it!" Pat cried, wanting to pinch herself to make sure the situation was real. "A million dollars," she whispered.

They were standing on the terrace that encircled the back of the house, looking out into the inky blackness of the cold, crisp New Mexico night. Pat wore her ermine wrap, but Blaise weathered the cold in just his suit. Directly behind the house was a smartly landscaped area with a gazebo and trees, which were not native to the land. Beyond that—desert. It gave one a feeling of being isolated. Only three stars winked down from a sky that held a quarter moon.

"I told you I didn't deal in thousands of dollars," Blaise said, leaning against the railing as he watched her.

"I know—but a million. How did you do it?" she asked, turning to him.

"I'm a wizard," he said with a laugh. "And you charmed the pants off old Houston."

"Pantless or not, the man wouldn't have promised to invest a million dollars if you hadn't approached him," Pat said honestly. "I'm very, very grateful."

"How grateful?" he asked, his tone making her nerve endings tingle.

A deep color came to her, which the night hid, mercifully. Pat looked down, sweeping lashes touching her face.

"No, no, Lady Pat. I'm not asking for a pound of flesh or your lovely, supple body in payment for anything I've done. That's not how I work," he said evenly. "If you come to me, you come out of your own volition, not out of gratitude." He touched her hair, slowly pulling out the two combs that held it back. The golden-brown tresses fell loose and free, framing her face and making her look like a sultry gypsy, but he made no move toward her, even though she caught herself wishing that he would.

"Did you ever stop to wonder, Patti, what would have happened in our lives if Aunt Delia hadn't come out on the terrace that time?" he asked, referring to her engagement party, when she had found herself alone with him on a terrace quite like this one. He had almost kissed her then.

Pat raised her head slightly. The thought had teased her mind every so often when she was alone at night, waiting for Roger to come home. "Nothing would have happened," she said quietly.

"If you say so," he said, his voice trailing off. But his tone gave lie to her words.

"I was engaged to Roger."

"Yes, but engagements have been broken," he replied in the same tone. "And you were so pretty, dressed in moonlight." He turned his eyes fully on her. "And now you're beautiful."

"I never know what to say," she replied honestly. "You keep giving me compliments and I—"

"—Should just say thank you," Blaise said. "That's all. 'Thank you.' It's not so hard," he said, running his finger over her lips, tracing the pattern of a kiss on them and giving her goosebumps in the process. Goosebumps, like a kid, she told herself, glad that she was wrapped in her fur piece so that he could not see the effect he had on her.

"It's getting colder," she said. "I'd better go in."

"I can warm you," he offered smoothly.

"You already have," she replied honestly. "I don't need a full-fledged fire."

"I think you do," he said, his voice trailing after Pat as she went inside.

Seven

Pat entered her bedroom with terribly mixed emotions. The dinner had been a triumph, and the Eagle was secure for at least a little while. That was all she had hoped for. Houston Fields was a man of his word—she knew that from all the things she had heard about him.

So why had she turned away at the last moment from the man who had arranged everything?

She looked in the mirror as she slowly got undressed, as if seeking an answer to her question from the face that looked back at her. Was it Roger's memory she was afraid of dishonoring? Was it still Blaise himself she did not fully trust? Or was it herself? Was she afraid to let love, or whatever this emotion actually was, take possession of her?

Without it, without Blaise in her life, there was only neat order, she thought as she slipped under the covers and sat up in the large, canopied bed with its delicate lace curtains opened at the sides and front. True, there was controversy, but nothing she was not up to. A romance with Blaise . . . well, that was something she was not quite sure about. She did not want to begin an affair knowing that someday it would end, as all his others had. So, she had better pull out the stops while she had any say in the matter, Pat told herself, trying to argue away the longing that she felt taking deeper and deeper hold of her.

She fluffed up the pillow behind her, and when she turned back around, Blaise was peering in through the unlocked French doors that led into her bedroom, having come around from his own terrace.

"Not alseep yet, I see," he said mildly, pushing open the door. "I approve," he said, his eyes on the blue lacy nightgown she wore. "I think blue's more your color."

"Just look at you, a grown man peeking into a woman's bedroom," Pat said, trying to sound stern, but not succeeding. She felt an excitement bubble up inside her despite all the determined words in her lecture of only a few seconds ago.

Blaise closed the door behind him. "Some of my best memories started by peeking into a woman's bedroom," he said, his smile inviting and broad. "Besides, I forgot to tell you."

"What?" she asked, cocking her head slightly and succeeding in looking both sweet and fetching at the same time. She caught her reflection in the mirrored closet doors by the side of her lounge chair and was pleased with the image. What nonsense, her more sensible side chided, yet she could not stop.

Blaise sat gingerly on the edge of the bed, raising his eyes to her in supposed supplication. "Am I permitted to advance toward the queen?"

"That depends on what you mean by advance," she bantered back.

His rich, throaty laugh sent a shiver all through her. "Anything I possibly can," he whispered, at once a young boy and a man of the world. "But for now," he said in a voice that was meant, she supposed, to put her at ease, "I just wanted to tell you about the country that came through."

Pat's eyes narrowed; the meanderings of her mind landed abruptly on earth. "Look, Blaise, if you need a ruse to stay here, I'd appreciate it if you'd pick something else," she said hotly. "I'll not have you belittling the significance of the Eagle or my involvement with it. And—"

"There really is someplace," Blaise stated simply, his expression having changed from surprise at her tirade to understanding to a seriousness that was unquestionably genuine.

"There really is someplace?" she echoed, bemused. Was it possible that he had not been teasing? It seemed unlikely that Blaise would have kept something this important from her for a whole day, but his level gaze indicated that he had spoken the truth. "Where then?" she asked.

He took her hands in his, and the gentle pressure was reassuring. "Canada."

She leaned back a little. "Canada?" she repeated. "But . . ."

"At the moment, our brothers to the north have close to one million unemployed, and the two hundred eighty-two souls in the House of Commons would like to remedy that situation—and to get themselves reelected. So, we are slated to meet with them next week and see about setting up a factory there to make your Eagles. In exchange for that, the Canadians will advance us thirty million dollars . . . if they like the deal," he added as an afterthought.

"Thirty million . . . thirty million dollars?" Pat stammered. This was too wonderful to be happening.

"If they like the deal," Blaise repeated, making it sound that he had absolutely no doubt about getting their approval.

"Blaise, you're a miracle worker!" Pat cried, staring at him in amazement.

"There has been talk of canonization," he acknowledged. "Hey, you're trembling. Easy, it's only money." He playfully tugged at the bow that laced together the front of her nightgown. "I'd rather you trembled that way because I'm so close to you, not because you got a measly thirty million dollars," he said, his eyes playing wickedly with her cleavage, which rose and fell inches away from him.

Pat's skin began to burn as she realized the situation she was in. "Um, perhaps you'd better leave . . ." she said, but her voice lacked conviction.

Blaise shook his dark head. "Nope. Uh-uh. Not a good idea at all."

"But I . . . I can't let you . . ." speaking seemed to require a great deal of effort as the bow became undone, exposing her soft breasts to his searing touch.

"Yes you can, if you try hard," Blaise said in a sultry voice that excited her all the more.

Her delicately polished fingertips tried just once to keep his head from lowering as his lips drew near her breasts. She felt her nipples grow harder in anticipation of his warm mouth and tongue.

"Blaise, I—"

He put his finger to her lips. "Shh. Why don't you stop all this small talk? I've got something better for your lips to do," he said, just before he covered her lips with his own.

There was something about the way his body pressed against hers, the feel of her breasts rubbing against the light covering of dark hair on his brawny chest, that caused a lightning ray of overwhelming agitation to shoot through her being. It was as if Pat had never been kissed before, never desired before, never had a man hold her before. This was all new, all wonderfully, passionately new.

Her body was on fire as she felt him caress her over and over. Then his hand slipped under the cover to find one shapely, tapered leg and inch its way maddeningly up, slowly, languidly, until it came to rest on her thigh, teasing her. She knew that he was well versed in his craft, knew that she should pull back before she fell headlong into something that she had no business letting happen, least of all now.

But it was too late to run for cover.

All her life she had dreamed of this feeling, not fully understanding it, not believing that it was possible. After marriage, she had convinced herself that it was a product of wistful romances and old movies. But it wasn't. It was real. This magic flashing through her over and over again made her desire more, made her blood run hot and her pulse threaten to explode. This was happening right now and nothing else mattered. There was no family schism, no children siding with her mother-in-law, no Hamilton jet demanding her time and endless energy. There was just Blaise and this wonderful, wondrous feeling.

She clung to him, entwining her fingers in the thick shock of his hair, loving the way it felt in her hands, loving the pattern that it traced along the nape of his neck.

"See, Patti," he said, his face just above hers, "you can if you try." He whispered the words against her cheek, then kissed her again, his mouth scorching her in its demand for her.

His tongue traced out the contours of her own as Pat realized that she had been freed of her nightgown and that his hot body was fitting against hers, rounding against the curves and filling out the hollows. He continued to heighten her desire until she thought she'd scream out his name and plead for him to take her. She had never before known such pleasure, never before known such a building of a climactic crescendo.

He took his time with her, as if leading a young girl to her first taste of love, and in a way, he was. He might not love her, but now she admitted to herself that all these years he had been a dream for her, buried deep in the caverns of her mind. He had been there since the first time his eyes took hold of her at the party. She had longed for him, had wanted to be his. It was an irrational, inexplicable emotion and Pat had denied its existence for twenty years. She loved Blaise Hamilton, always had, always would. It had been too late for her from the very first meeting. The rhythm of their lovemaking grew frenzied, and suddenly the world exploded for Pat as she wildly called Blaise's name.

The lights twinkled and faded as she returned to her canopied bed in her house in the outskirts of Albuquerque, New Mexico. But the wondrous journey was not over. Blaise's arms were still around her, and his kisses, now soft and tender, were gently covering the outline of her cheek and neck. She realized that the heavy breathing, which she had thought was her own, was partly his as the rhythmic sound grew steadier.

"No, Patti, you are definitely not 'past' it," Blaise said with a small laugh. "What a fool Roger was," he murmured softly, his fingers tracing a pattern between her breasts and gliding along her taut, flat stomach. "I would have sold a dozen factories for one night like this with you," he said, and there was no mocking, teasing tone to his words.

His touch began to arouse her again, igniting the fires that dwelled beneath her skin's surface, and she heard herself say, "The night's not over yet."

Blaise raised himself on one elbow, looking down at her. She could not understand the look in his eyes. "No," he whispered, "it's not." And he took her into his arms once more.

Pat was not sure how to face him the next morning, for she had never had a lover before, never been loved by anyone except Roger. So when she found Blaise in the kitchen, it was by accident, for part of her was afraid that he would treat it all as a joke.

But his behavior was no different than it had been before they had made love. His look was light, though his eyes held more familiarity than they had yesterday.

"I thought you'd never get up," he said, offering her a glass of orange juice that Angelica had set out.

Pat sipped it cautiously as she watched him. "Do you know you look pretty in the morning without makeup?" Blaise asked.

"Shh!" Pat chided, glancing at Angelica to see if the woman had heard. She caught a glimpse of a smile on the woman's round face as Angelica went on preparing Pat's breakfast at the far side of the kitchen.

"What are you ashamed of?" Blaise lowered his voice to a loud stage whisper. "Men and women do this sort of thing all the time, you know. That's how other little men and women come about—or hasn't anyone explained that to you?" he asked. "I'd be happy to give you a quick refresher course."

"You are impossible," Pat said, thinking that the remark sounded as if it came from an old movie.

He chucked her under the chin fondly. "No, just eager, Patti." He rose to leave, taking his jacket under his arm. "I'm going to make arrangements for a flight to Ottawa," he explained as her eyes questioned his departure. He patted her hand. "Don't worry, I'll be back. I never leave a tigress waiting too long."

Pat felt a blush rising to her cheeks, and Blaise's

deep laugh rang in her ears. She glanced up to see Anglica stealing glances at her, grinning.

"Angelica," Pat said, almost hiding behind her juice glass as she raised it for another sip, "whatever you're thinking—don't."

"Housekeepers are not paid to think," Angelica replied, but Pat could tell from her tone that the well-rounded woman was pleased.

Pat's euphoric state lasted until three o'clock that afternoon, when Sara came home. Her daughter was attending the University of New Mexico and lived on campus, an arrangement that had at first saddened Pat, and then, when the trouble over the will had started, had become a relief.

"What are you doing home?" Pat asked, hoping that her daughter's visit signaled a change of heart. She hated being separated from her and Bucky over the Eagle, hated their viewing her as a pawn. She had always believed that her children had thought of her as her own person. Obviously, she did not know them as well as she thought she did.

"Uncle Jonathan called me at school," Sara said, her voice brittle.

She looked like a female version of her father— the same wide face, the same nose, not quite small, but with a dignity to it. Her frame was larger than Pat's, and she was taller, even though she wore flats and Pat was in heels. How could she look so much like Roger and not have some of his feelings? Pat wondered for the thousandth time since the schism had started.

"Oh?" Pat said, indicating with her eyes that

Sara should sit next to her on the living-room sofa. Sara chose to take a chair opposite her mother instead.

"He asked me to try to talk some sense into you one last time before the trial," Sara said, her gaze unwavering.

"Not above turning the knife a little more in the wound, is he?" Pat asked, then regretted the bitterness of her words.

"Oh, Mother, don't be so melodramatic. Uncle Jonathan and Grandmother just want you not to make a fool of yourself over this thing before it's too late."

"And what do you think?" Pat pressed, hoping against hope to hear something different from her daughter. If only now, at the eleventh hour, her daughter could be moved to join her, then Pat's victory would be complete. She knew that whatever Sara decided, Bucky would naturally join in. They were very close that way.

"Why, I agree with them, of course," Sara said in haughty surprise. "Why else would I be here?"

"Why else indeed," Pat echoed, rising. "I thought perhaps it was just to visit your mother."

"Don't you start on guilt," Sara said highhandedly.

Pat whirled on her firstborn with angry eyes. "Then don't you start making impossible demands," she said. "This project was something your father believed in, and I promised to see it through—and so I will. Neither you, nor Jonathan, nor Rose is going to stop me!"

Sara lifted her chin. She looked a little like a bull terrier, digging in, Pat thought sadly. It was a look Roger had worn when things were particularly tough. "Act your age, Mother. You can't do this alone."

"I'm not doing this alone. Your cousin Blaise is helping me," Pat said with a touch of triumph. Someone in the family sided with her!

"Cousin Blaise?" Sara said, her voice disparaging despite the fact that the last time she had seen him she was no more than six, and could have no real memories of him, Pat was sure. Except, perhaps, the ones that Mother Rose and the others fed her. "Now you're letting *him* lead you around by the nose?"

That tore it. "You listen to me, young lady. I don't know what's happened to your mind, or your eyes, but if you'd open up both, you'd see that no one leads me where I have no desire to be led. And as for my age, missy, I'm a hell of a lot younger than you are!" she said with outraged dignity. "Because I can give credence to visions while all you can see is the mud and the mire!"

The sound of applause was heard from the top of the living-room steps. Pat jerked her head around to see Blaise standing there, nodding his approval.

"Very well put," he said genially, coming into the room and putting one hand on Pat's shoulder while extending the other toward Sara. "Hello, Sara," he said.

Stiffly, the plainly dressed girl shook his hand, a scowl on her face.

"Well, you've got Jonathan's handshake, that's for sure," Blaise said, looking at the limp hand in his.

Sara's face sank deeper into a scowl as she pulled her hand away abruptly. "You're making a terrible mistake, Mother, if you're listening to him," she said, nodding insolently at Blaise. "You're going to lose everything and make us a laughing stock as well," she snapped.

Pat was embarrassed by Sara's behavior toward Blaise and infuriated that her daughter still thought of her as someone's pawn, be it Blaise's or Roger's.

"On the contrary, he is listening to me—which is why I have his support. Get it through your head, Sara, no one is manipulating me. And no one's going to manipulate me!" she said with finality, glancing at both Sara and Blaise, in case he had thoughts to the contrary after last night.

Sara turned on her heel in a huff and left the house as abruptly as she had entered it.

"Well," Pat sighed, "that was a short visit. I'm sorry about her behavior," she said ruefully. "I did raise her to have manners—I also raised her to have clearer sight. I seem to have failed in both," she said, shaking her head sadly as she looked in the direction of her departed daughter.

Blaise took her in his arms gently, with no intention other than comfort. "They don't always turn out the way you bend them, no matter how good your example. But Sara's young, she might come around yet," he said optimistically.

"In the meantime, I have a court battle to prove I'm not crazy in believing in Roger's plane," Pat said wearily.

"If you are, then the Prime Minister of Canada is crazy and so is Houston Fields. Now, I don't know about you," he said with a twinkle in his eyes, "but I wouldn't want to be the judge to tell the rich old man that he's crazy, would you?" he asked.

Pat laughed a little in response. "No, I guess not."

"Better, much better. I said you looked pretty without makeup, but a sad look certainly does dress you down. Keep those frowns at bay, hear?" he said, touching her cheek fondly.

"Yes, sir," she said, saluting.

"That's right," Blaise nodded in approval, "the proper respect at all times and we'll get along fine," he teased. "Did you mean what you said about not being led where you didn't want to go?" he asked.But his manner told Pat that he already knew the answer and merely wanted her to reaffirm it for him.

Her attitude became a little cooler as she thought of her independence. At the moment, it was the only thing she was sure of. "If you mean last night, yes, I came to you willingly, and yes, it was wonderful, but it doesn't mean that there are any obligations between us or that I'm letting you take over."

Blaise shook his head, and she was at a loss to know whether her words angered him or merely amused him. "You're a tough cookie, Lady Pat. Would you like my lawyers to draw up a preaffair agreement?" he asked, letting a smile come to his lips, but it was a smile tinged with bitterness.

"There isn't going to be an 'affair,' Blaise," Pat said, turning to leave the room. It sounded so cold, calling it an affair. What she had had last night was something special, something no one else had ever had before. She didn't want to pin a common label on it.

Blaise caught her arm and turned her back around. His eyes were intense as he looked down into her face. "There already is one," he said, his voice quiet, not matching his expression.

Shaken, Pat withdrew.

But Pat did not have much time to contemplate her private life. The phone rang several minutes after Blaise left, and it was Sam, reporting that someone had broken in and stolen one of the specialized parts of the gas turbine engines.

All the way to the plant, Pat's head ached with conjectures and indecisions. Whom was she to trust? Was someone within the plant betraying her? Or someone from the outside? With all her heart, she fervently prayed it was the latter.

"We'll have to get a new part," Pat said to Sam after surveying the area from which the item had been taken. The door to the factory had been jimmied open and it was only after the security guard had discovered it that Sam and Pardy had been called in. Sam had called Pat as soon as he had assessed what had happened.

"That's going to take time," Sam said, shaking his head.

Pat turned desperately to the foreman. "Can a new one be made instead?" she asked.

The barrel-chested man scratched his head as he rolled the thought over in his mind. "I don't think so."

"But you've got the specifications," Pat urged. "They were written up just last Friday. If we called in Bill and Dale," she said, naming the head engineers, "and they did it with the help of the reliability section . . ." She turned to Sam, who, unlike Pardy, nodded his agreement.

"It's worth a try," he said. "Better than standing around and scratching our heads," he said rather deliberately, and Pardy glared at Sam, obviously taking offense at his words.

Pat knew that Sam did not like the foreman, had never liked him, but Pardy had been with them a long time, longer even than Sam, so she tried to keep the peace.

"All right," she said to Sam, "call them." She turned to Pardy, knowing that the man took any unintended slight as an insult to his authority. "Work with them, Wade. If anyone can get us through this, you can," she said, and the ruddy-faced man gave her a quick smile before he went off to his office.

"Something's not right, boss lady," Sam said when she turned back to him.

"You mean other than just everything?" Pat said, her voice echoing through the huge, barnlike, gray-walled production area.

"Whoever broke in knew just what they were looking for," Sam said. "They didn't waste time with petty destruction. They went right for the heart of the plane."

Pat closed her eyes. "I know what you're saying," she said heavily. It was an inside job—there was no fooling themselves about that. Sam was just her Greek chorus, reiterating what she knew was true. "Get more security guards. The ones Blaise hired for us aren't enough," she said ruefully.

"What are you going to be doing?" Sam asked, not standing on ceremony.

"I'm going to be getting ready to go to Canada

to lie and tell those people that everything is going smoothly, that our plane can not only fly but do tricks, and that we will meet the deadline we hemmed ourselves into at that press conference," she said with a bewildered sigh.

Sam's gaunt, dark face studied her closely, his thoughts masked from her, as always.

Eight

"What's bothering you?" Blaise asked as they left the plane. Carrying the two carry-on suitcases that comprised their only luggage, he guided Pat toward the exit at the far side of the busy airport. "All during the trip you've seemed preoccupied—and hostile."

"You're imagining things," Pat said, dismissing his statement airily while she kept her eyes averted.

"Lady, if there's one thing I can spot, it's a hostile woman. Now you'd better pull yourself together for the Prime Minister. He doesn't care for scowling women—and neither do I," Blaise added. "What's the matter? Did I overstep another boundary again?" he asked. This time he sounded a bit annoyed.

They had spent the long journey from New Mexico's Municipal Airport to Ottawa Uplands Airport mostly in silence, as Pat mulled over the entire situation. Someone was obviously betraying her and she didn't know whom to suspect. No one within the factory, or "the Family" as she had come to think of them all, stood to gain anything if the Eagle never made it off the ground.

"Is that a smile, or just gas?" Blaise asked, taking her arm as they stepped outside. The cold November wind whipped at Pat's ermine hood, pushing the pile forward against her face.

"Do you always word things so eloquently?" she asked as the wind snatched at her breath, making her lungs ache. A few snowflakes fell against her cheek. The remains of the last snowstorm were around her fashionable, knee-high boots as Pat leaned against Blaise to steady her walk.

"Well, it got a response, didn't it?" Blaise said with a chuckle. "Besides, I don't recall you having that kind of look on your face before. Ah, a coach and four," he muttered as a taxi pulled up slowly in front of them.

Blaise bundled her inside and she moved awkwardly toward the window, leaving room for him. The taxi felt oppressively warm from its old heater and Pat let her coat part.

"Chateau Laurier," Blaise said to the driver, then settled back next to Pat, putting his arm easily around her shoulders.

Pat had the feeling that he had done this countless times before in hundreds of taxicabs, whisking a woman off to an elegantly furnished room. Well, she was not about to be sidetracked.

"That's not the name of the Prime Minister's residence," she pointed out.

Blaise laughed, and she felt a little like a child who had said something amusing. He shook his head, his eyes snapping invitingly at her, showing her that part of him was not thinking about business at all.

"I'm not that important, Lady Pat. I couldn't wangle us an invitation with the Prime Minister. But I did manage to get a room at the most expensive hotel in town, despite the heavy flow of conventioneers—which, I hope you appreciate, is no mean trick. Despite this being the capital, Ottawa does not have that many places to stay once conventions really get started."

But all Pat heard was one word.

"Room?" she repeated.

His eyes sparkled merrily. "Have to economize in some way," he said softly. "Our President requests it."

"I want two rooms," she said firmly.

"Where's your patriotism?" he asked, amused, pushing back her hood after he had taken off his fur-lined gloves. His warm hand brushed against her face, making her tingle.

"Tucked behind my good sense," Pat replied, glancing out the window and watching the scenery go by. Ottawa was a combination of old and new, with Victorian buildings existing comfortably alongside modern structures. A layer of snow lay where, in the summer, a myriad of bright flowers peered back at tourists.

"A pity," Blaise said, his voice a trace harder to Pat's ear. "But I'm afraid your good sense will have to take into account the fact that there are no other rooms available at the moment."

Pat turned back to Blaise. "That's impossible," she said. This wasn't the backwoods, this was the capital of Canada. Surely there had to be "a room at the inn," she thought.

As if reading her thoughts, Blaise took his arm from her shoulders and said, "There might be a stable or two available, but the town is full up. There're twenty separate conventions taking place here," he said. "And all those conventioneers are wondering if they're in for another snowstorm," he added, glancing past her out the window.

It sounded impossible, but she had no doubt that he was speaking the truth. Blaise would have researched something like that. Despite her resolve, she felt overjoyed at being "forced" to spend the night with him. But something within her pulled back, ever watchful. It was vital that she sever all contact with the part of her that was vulnerable. A lot more was at stake here than just her heart, which had already been lost in the gamble.

"I could sleep on the sofa the way they did in the old movies," he whispered, winking gallantly. His breath made her shiver as it tickled her cheek.

The taxi stopped at Confederation Square in front of the 1912 edifice that played host to all the important dignitaries who passed through Canada.

"Are we here?"

"That we are," Blaise said, leaning forward to pay the driver the fare plus a handsome tip. The man stammered his thanks for the extra twenty in his hand as he nearly tripped over himself to get out, come around and open Pat's door.

"I thought we were economizing," Pat whispered against her fur hood, looking up at Blaise as she stepped out of the cab.

Blaise grinned. "You've nothing against being

generous to the less fortunate, have you?" he asked.

She had to smile as she shook her head, not in answer to his question but in response to the deviltry in his eyes. The man had a way of squirming out of everything. She could see how he managed to wheel and deal so well.

Blaise whisked her inside quickly, out of the cold, which was beginning to nip at her despite her heavy, calf-length ermine coat. Immediately, a sense of elegant warmth surrounded her in the lobby of the hotel, which had been named after Prime Minister Sir Wilfrid Laurier. The lobby was filled to capacity, but even the conventioneers, recognizable because of their badges, seemed sufficiently subdued by the luxurious atmosphere.

"See?" Blaise said, in case Pat still doubted him. "You're lucky we don't have to double up with a couple from Lower Sandusky, California," he said as they reached the desk.

He gave his name to the austere man at the front desk, who seemed to come alive at the mere mention of it. A bellhop appeared at their elbow from out of thin air, and within a few minutes Blaise and Pat were standing in an elegant, ornate suite.

"I've seen smaller guesthouses," Pat said, looking around the front room.

Despite the large size of the room, once the bellhop had left, clutching his tip and trying to appear unaffected but not succeeding, Pat felt very, very alone with Blaise.

He watched her for a long moment as she looked at the view—or tried to. All she really was conscious of was that they were alone together.

Blaise came up behind her as she stood in the doorway of the bedroom and slowly slipped her fur coat from her shoulders and tossed it onto the bed.

"So," Pat said with effort, finding a voice that wanted to be still, "when do we see the Prime Minister?"

Blaise's lips found the hollow of her throat and Pat struggled to remember why she was here. The Eagle, the Eagle, her mind echoed in diminishing tones.

"Who?" Blaise asked as his lips slowly trailed around her neck and up against her ear, his tongue encircling the outline ever so lightly.

"The . . . Prime . . . Minister . . ." Pat fought to get the words out of the swirling sea that was engulfing her brain.

"Oh, him," Blaise murmured, his voice teasing as his fingers began to undo the buttons of her bone-white suit jacket. "We'll call him later," he promised, his flesh making contact with hers.

With strength that came out of nowhere, Pat stepped back, fighting her way out of the hot haze around her. "We'll call him now," she said. "It wouldn't do to keep him waiting."

Fool, her mind echoed.

But Blaise seemed to take it all in stride as he shrugged and calmly went to the old-fashioned white telephone that stood on the nightstand. He dialed a number without consulting his telephone book, then, after a quiet exchange that lasted barely three minutes, he hung up and turned back to Pat, who had used the time to compose herself.

"I'm afraid we're out of luck."

"What?" Pat exclaimed suspiciously.

"Seems that an emergency came up. He won't be able to see us until tomorrow," Blaise said.

"And what will tomorrow's excuse be? Canada's gone to war?" she asked with a tinge of cynicism.

"If they go to war, they'll probably need the planes that much faster," he said glibly. He stepped over to her again, and instead of being angry, he looked at her with understanding, pity, and a trace of sadness. "Patti, when did you lose that innocent trust you had?" he asked, slowly rebuttoning her jacket for her.

His gesture filled her with a tender feeling for him, which she tried to banish. It was just what he wanted, her logical mind told her. He wanted to keep her guard down and her resistance low, so he could manipulate her. "When I became chairman of the board and responsible to a lot of other people," she said truthfully.

"C'mon," he said with a small sigh. "Let me take the chairman of the board to lunch, and then we'll take in the sights." After a pause, he offered invitingly, "Unless you want to stay here."

Yes, she wanted to stay here. She wanted to be made love to again, but it was the last thing she could allow herself to do. "Lunch will be wonderful," she said, picking up her coat.

"No, lunch will be fine. Something else will be wonderful," he promised, a wicked glint coming into his eye.

How well he knew his women, she thought. She held her head high as she passed him out the door. Was it her imagination, or did she hear him chuckle to himself?

They had lunch at the hotel's sedate yet charming Canadian Grill; then, seeing that the weather had let up a little, Blaise escorted Pat out and proposed that they do what women liked to do second best.

"Which is?" Pat asked archly.

"Shop," he said innocently.

"And what is it in your estimation that women like to do first?" she asked gamely as the elegant-looking doorman hailed a cab for them. The frosty chill in the air had died away, and while the pregnant clouds still hovered over them, no more snowflakes descended for the moment.

Blaise grinned widely at her. "If your memory's so poor, I suggest we retire back up to the suite and I'll remind you," he said, snuggling close to her as the doorman closed the cab door behind them.

Her coat made it difficult to slide over when she felt the outline of Blaise's hard, muscular leg against hers, despite the many layers of clothing between them. She had to get control of herself!

"I think you're oversimplifying things," she said, gathering her dignity around her.

"I think you're overcomplicating them," he countered. "You're the last person I would have thought capable of indulging in games."

"I'm not the one playing games. You've got to admit," Pat said, letting her guard down for a moment and speaking to him the way she wanted to, "your reputation with women makes it a little difficult to take anything you say without a grain of salt."

"Perhaps Lady Pat can't," he said seriously. "But Patti can," he added with a whisper that recalled their night of love.

Pat turned from him, confused. She didn't want

to risk a major disappointment by daring to hope that he was serious about her. But as the tender, wonderful, endless moments of lovemaking shimmered vividly before her, she could not believe that this was something he went through mechanically. How could all that have happened between them without any feelings on his part? And yet, how could there be any? He had an army of women at his beck and call, far more experienced, far more sophisticated than she.

"You're thinking too hard," Blaise chided, his deep voice breaking into her thoughts. "The vein in your forehead is standing out," he said, his fingers brushing against it as if to smooth it back. "Let everything happen the way it should," he advised.

"I fully intend to," she said, thinking of the Eagle and her promise to Roger.

"Good," he said, settling back in the deep seat of the cab, obviously not thinking of the Eagle at all.

The cab driver took them to the Sparks Street Mall, an outdoor shopping area comprised of five city blocks filled with shops, both thriving department stores and little boutiques that brought the word *quaint* to mind immediately. In addition, there were historic buildings, rock gardens, sculptures galore, and even a few brave musicians who provided live entertainment as they stood around a heater donated by the department store that had hired them. The four violinists took turns playing and warming themselves at the heater.

"This is a more interesting place in the summer," Blaise said as he escorted Pat into the store.

"Of course, then you have to deal with the heat. It gets pretty bad here at times."

"A little heat would be nice now," Pat commented, feeling her face tingle as the warmth of the store met it.

"I could take care of that," Blaise volunteered.

"Don't you ever stop?" she asked with a laugh.

"Not until they bury me," he said honestly. "Ah, women's wear," he read from the directory. "Let's go."

"Why do you think you know my tastes?" she asked as he directed her exactly where she would normally have gone.

"Because, Lady Pat, I know everything about you."

And he seemed to.

It was almost eerie. Blaise knew her favorite color. At lunch, he had ordered for her without asking her and had known just what she would have chosen on the menu. He knew her favorite drink. And the suite had been decorated in her favorite colors. And now he chose a cocktail dress that her own instincts would have led her to had he not been there. How careful a study had he made of her? she wondered as he urged her to try on the dress. And why?

Pat modeled the navy chiffon cocktail dress and saw the approval in Blaise's eyes as she turned with the full skirt swinging out around her. She was proud of the way the dress nipped in at her waist. She felt sensual in it. The dress had long full sleeves and the front had a deep, deep V neck that disappeared into the wide belt. She felt as if she were wearing an airy, floating cloud.

"We'll take it," Blaise said, looking at the sales-person who was hovering.

The elderly, refined-looking woman smiled se-renely as she nodded her approval.

Neither she nor Blaise was present when Pat came back out with the dress resting prettily on a hanger. Pat glanced around and saw Blaise by the lingerie counter, paying for an item. He spotted her looking at him, then picked up the round, aqua gift box that contained his purchase and came over to her.

"Anything else you want?" he asked.

She shook her head, wondering for whom he had made the purchase. Was there a special girl friend lurking somewhere in his life? An extra-special woman who could put up with his con-sorting with so many women? She would have to be made of tough mettle, Pat thought, as Blaise helped her back on with her coat.

They spent another hour shopping, then Blaise took her back to the hotel. Was he in a hurry to get on with his tryst before he met someone else here? she pondered all the way back in the cab. After all, he was no stranger to this city, and, like a sailor, he probably had a girl in every port.

Or under every rock, she thought cynically, then reproached herself. She was here on business. Hadn't she backed away from his offer of love this afternoon? Wasn't she afraid of being bedded by him tonight? Afraid, because her attachment would only grow. Well, what did she want? To have him and not to have him?

What she wanted, Pat realized, was to have the Eagle's responsibility stripped from her—never to have had the Eagle exist in the first place—and to enjoy this time between them. But if not for the Eagle, Blaise would never have "ridden in to her rescue" in the first place, she reminded herself. It was a dilemma no matter which way she approached it.

"Hurry and change," Blaise said as they walked back into the suite at the hotel.

"Why?"

"I've never met such a suspicious woman," he said with a laugh. "And you look so easygoing, too."

"Nature's way of compensating," she said flippantly, still waiting for an answer. She watched him put down the round gift box almost carelessly as he handed her her new cocktail dress, which he had insisted on paying for.

"We're going to the theater," he said.

"The theater? When did you have time to—?"

"Arrangements all made well in advance. I leave nothing to chance," he said.

"Then you knew the Prime Minister wouldn't see us today," she accused.

"No, I didn't know that," he denied, sounding surprised at her suggestion. "But I didn't think he'd hold us prisoner at Parliament Hill at night, either. And I thought you needed a little public diversion," he said, brushing a curl that fell into her face. "I'll provide the private diversion later," he promised.

She cocked her head. "Think so?"

His smile was mysterious. "I thought I understood women, but some of the time, Lady Pat, I'm not quite sure I know what you're driving at." He paused, then his eyes took on a boyish gleam. "Well?"

"Well what?" she asked guardedly, still holding the package in her hands.

"Do you change into that, or do I do it for you?" he suggested, already taking the package from her.

Her eyes darted toward the open door of the bedroom, then back at Blaise. "Do I get my privacy?" she asked.

"More than you really want," he said.

She walked off quickly, annoyance evident in her gait. Why did he have to be so smug and self-confident? Couldn't he leave her with a little bit of pride and dignity? He had said no games, but he could at least let her hide her longing for him behind a facade. His confidence made her angry. Slipping into the soft new dress, she resolved to keep Blaise at bay. There was no putting him in his place, since she hadn't the vaguest notion where his place was. She had a strong hunch that even Mother Rose would have played into his hands if she was assured that no one would know. Even ice water turned to hot blood in the veins of any woman who was around Blaise Hamilton.

After brushing her hair carefully, Pat put in two decorative clips to keep the honey-brown mane off her face, then picked up the clutch purse that Blaise had bought for her, and walked out a proud but nervous warrior, sorely underarmed.

Nine

The cab dropped them off in front of one of the National Arts Centre's three theaters as the evening air became more brisk and made Pat long for home. New Mexico's winters were cold too, but she was unaccustomed to the dampness, and it chilled her to the bone.

"They're playing *Star Bright*," Blaise said before she had an opportunity to look at the marquee. Actually, the wind had gotten so blustery that Pat didn't even want to look up, only get inside as quickly as possible.

Pat looked surprised at his declaration. "The play that just left Broadway?" she asked, waiting for a moment to let the warmth of the theater seep in while she stood on the rich, red carpet in the lobby.

Blaise nodded, pulling off his camel-colored gloves as he fished in his breast pocket for the tickets to hand to the usher. "A lot of touring companies pass through here," he said. "I thought you might like to see a musical again."

Again. He knew she liked musicals. They were her favorite form of play and she hadn't seen one since, oh, six months before Roger had died. She had gone with Sara. The last bit of mother-daughter fun they had shared before the flare-up, Pat thought with a pang.

Her brown eyes looked up into Blaise's rugged face, which now looked tender and solicitous. "Ready?" he asked. "The curtain's about to go up."

She nodded, and for the next two hours everything melted away into songs and laughter. It felt wonderful.

"You should do things like that more often," Blaise said over his drink at the Faces nightclub.

Despite the din, it felt very intimate right now. Must be the drink, Pat thought. He should have taken her to dinner first, then a drink, she thought, feeling a bit fuzzy.

"I haven't the time," she said vaguely, although in her mind she agreed with him.

"You should take the time to enjoy life," he said. "It doesn't wait for you to catch up. A year and a half is a long time to stay away from the theater when you enjoy it so much."

Pat put down her drink and tried to focus on his eyes in the dim light. "I'm beginning to think you've had a little man stashed under my bed, watching my every move."

He laughed and she heard every delicious note

despite the wall of noise around them. "If I had, it would have been me, and I wouldn't have been *under* your bed, I would have been *in* it," he said, his eyes caressing her, sliding down slowly from her face to her rounded cleavage, which strained against the chiffon.

Pat cast her eyes down. "Yes, well—Blaise, about the sleeping arrangements—" she began almost nervously, her mind annoyed with her wavering attitude. Either accept it like an adult, or tell him no like an adult. Why hem and haw like a bewildered schoolgirl?

Blaise put his finger to her lips. "Shh. Things have a way of working themselves out," he said. "C'mon, it's time to feed you," he said with a gentle laugh, and she found herself on her feet, being cocooned in her ermine coat and almost carried out into the cold night.

Snowflakes were beginning to fall again.

Half an hour later, she was in his arms, dancing to dreamy music provided by a large orchestra at the Canadian Grill. She felt as if she could be molded against his body forever, floating along, being taken care of. . . . No, that's not what she wanted anymore. She was finally master of her own destiny. But her will ran into a lot of opposition provided by the wine and by the wonderful, seductive atmosphere of the club.

Pat barely remembered eating, although the fare was delicious, her faraway taste buds told her. The lobster was perfect, and Blaise had made some sort of smiling remark about not thinking he was overstepping his boundaries by cracking it for her and making dinner a little less messy.

When the waitress provided the bib that went

with the lobster dinner, Blaise had risen to tie it around Pat's neck, somehow managing to touch her throat, his sure fingers gliding down on the pretext of straightening out the bib. An overwhelming ache sprang up within her, yearning for his touch to go on.

And he sensed it. She could see by the light in his eyes that he knew. And she was helpless to change anything.

"Why are you trying to get me drunk?" she asked, for a bottle of champagne had been left at their table and Blaise made sure that her glass was never empty.

"I'm trying to make sure you relax," he said lightly.

"If I was any more relaxed," she murmured, "my bones would be liquid."

He laughed and Pat smiled at her own words, but then Blaise shook his head. "No, Lady Pat, you're still watching me, expecting me to pounce on you, expecting—I'm not sure what."

"You're imagining things," she replied, averting her face. Was she that transparent? Well, the C.I.A. would never call on her to do their counterintelligence work, she thought.

"I hope so," he said, putting his finger under her chin and bringing her eyes back to meet his. "Would you like to go upstairs now?" he asked.

No, no. Let's stay here, she thought she said in panic. But her lips weren't moving. Instead, her legs were. Somehow, she was walking in front of him, going toward the elevator, then toward the door of their room. Their *room*. It was going to happen again. One more time paradise would open up to her. There was no Prime Minister. No government contract. No loan. No, think about it later. Later. Right now, he wants you, her mind echoed almost outside of her brain as the carpet moved beneath her feet, bringing her ever closer to the bedroom.

Blaise's strong hands seemed to burn through the airy chiffon around her arms, caressing her, pulling her soul out to meet him. He turned her around to face him and removed the clips from her hair, then ran his fingers through the silky mane.

Pat wondered if he felt her tremble beneath his touch and realized that of course he did. He was well versed in this sort of thing, knowing just which button to press to cause a woman to fall helplessly into his arms. And she was no different, no different at all, she thought with despair— and with mounting desire.

He brought his lips to her neck, leaving a gentle trail of kisses from there to her low décolletage.

Pat put her arms around his neck and felt herself raised off the floor with a gesture so effortless that it seemed as if she weighed nothing at all. Her clothes seemed to melt away magically.

Suddenly, the bed was beneath her and he was above her, once again transporting her to another galaxy. She was insatiably hungry for the heady, wonderful world that only Blaise could give her. Her emotions swept her away, and she clung to Blaise, kissing him back over and over again. Material slid away from his body. They were swaddled then only in an overpowering need to love and be loved.

Heat was everywhere as Blaise took her, first fiercely, and later gently, feeding every need she had ever experienced. He cherished her and devoured her passion, mingling it with his own.

To be born sensually at forty was a nerve-shattering experience that had no equal, no name. A flood of gratitude filled Pat's heart as she realized her discovery was something that was absent from many women's lives. Before Blaise, she had not known the euphoria of surrendering to love. She was free from conscious thought, rejoicing on a plane closer to heaven than to earth.

Pat opened her eyes, her head resting against Blaise's shoulder, her heart beating madly against his hard chest. She felt no embarrassment at her nudity or his.

"Is this the end of my evening's entertainment?" she heard herself ask in a voice that strived to be light. Mustn't let him know how deeply she cared, how much she craved him.

The smile on Blaise's face made him look like the most charming devil anyone could have fashioned with an artist's brush, she thought.

"If you're up to it, Patti, this is only the beginning of your evening—your long evening," he whispered into her hair as his fingers caressed the length of her body possessively, gently playing with the inside of her thigh, arousing her once again. Arousing himself again, she thought as she felt the hard contours of his body yearn for her once more.

Pat turned to him. "You're incredible," she said with a great deal of affection.

"What have I been telling you all along?" He pulled himself up on his elbow and looked down into her face. "I intend to be the most incredible man in your life. I should have been that a long,

long time ago," he murmured as his lips parted hers, seeking, discovering; and Pat felt the heat of his rugged body grow and grow, enveloping her in its passion.

She clung to him and the fragments of his words as she felt his weight shift and roll onto her. Ecstasy beckoned once again and everything was set on fire—everything but his words, which managed to resound over and over again in her brain. Did it mean he actually cared? Or was that just for the benefit of the moment? She shouldn't take the chance. . . .

Within moments, none of this mattered at all.

Pat watched him reach out for her as she stood at the foot of the bed, dressed and ready to meet the Prime Minister. She had tried to reach Sam earlier that morning, but there was no one to take her call, which confirmed her suspicions that all was definitely not well—that, plus the fact that the Prime Minister mysteriously could not meet with them.

Perhaps Blaise had misrepresented the Canadian government's interest in the Eagle so that he could enjoy a brief fling with her here. Though he had already been fantastically helpful to her in generating funds, he had treated the project casually on several occasions, seeming not to understand the importance of her commitment.

But seeing Blaise sleeping there, in the bed they had shared last night, made her soul beg for a sign with which to believe in him. He looked totally guileless, lying there like that, only a small piece of the blue sheet covering his maleness. She felt herself becoming aroused again.

What was happening to her? Love was not supposed to be the most important part of her life anymore.

Pat walked over to Blaise, attempting to pull the cover over him a little more, when he suddenly opened his eyes and grabbed her wrist playfully. "Trying to sneak a peek while I sleep?" he asked mischievously. "For shame."

Pat felt color rise to her cheeks beneath her makeup and her olive complexion. "You were kicking it off," she said, trying not to sound embarrassed.

"Would that have been so bad?" he asked teasingly, sitting up.

"You'd better get dressed," she said, her voice amused at his ploy. She hoped she sounded sufficiently detached. "It's getting late."

"Okay," he said, getting up and moving like a well-trained athlete. Pat averted her eyes a moment later—not quite quickly enough not to see him. Blaise caught the motion. "Didn't seem to bother you last night," he commented, padding on bare feet to the shower.

"You have a way of constantly embarrassing me," she called into the bathroom. "Do you enjoy it?"

"In a way," he replied above the rush of the water. "But not nearly as much as I enjoy making love to you."

"Do we have to talk about that now?" she asked, uncomfortable. She had thought of herself as a modern woman, but he had a way of changing all that. He had a way of giving the lie to all the things she thought she knew about herself.

"No," he said, coming out as he toweled himself dry after an incredibly short shower. "We could be *doing* something about it instead," he suggested.

"Get dressed," she said, turning away and walking to the next room.

"Can't trust yourself, eh?" he chuckled.

Pat did not answer.

Her suspicions grew as, over breakfast, a now suavely dressed Blaise informed her that the Prime Minister was entirely unavailable. Her gaze hardened. So it *had* been a sham, she thought as her appetite failed her.

"Then I guess we had better take the next plane home," she said, putting down her coffee cup. "Unless you need to keep me here longer for some reason," she said cuttingly, her voice cold. How could he have used her like this?

The light in Blaise's shimmering blue eyes was annoyance, but he said nothing as he finished his coffee, then paused for a moment, as if to calm something inside. "If you take the plane now, the press here is going to be mighty annoyed with you. Not to mention those out-of-work Canadians."

She looked at him blankly, trying to clear the fog out of her mind. "What are you talking about?" she asked as a waitress appeared to refill her coffee cup. Pat placed her hand over it to stop her, but the woman was far too engrossed with Blaise's profile to take note and began to pour the hot liquid over Pat's hand.

She yelped in surprise and pain and the waitress jumped back in embarrassment. Blaise was quick to dip his handkerchief into the glass of ice water at his place and bathe Pat's red fingers.

"Wounded without even firing a shot," he said lightly, stroking her red fingers.

"Yes," she said, not thinking of the coffee at all as their eyes met and held for a moment.

"Well, you were asking me about my statement," Blaise said after a pause, his voice cutting through the electrically charged air. "The Prime Minister can't meet with us, but some very able representatives of his in the House of Commons can," he said. "Right after we hold a press conference."

"Another press conference?" she asked in dismay as the frightened young waitress appeared with a bowl of ice cubes.

"Yes, I'm afraid so," Blaise said, rising to help her on with her coat. "That's not necessary," he said to the waitress. "The lady has decided she'll live." He turned back to Pat. "Haven't you?"

Pat smiled, relieved that he had not lied to her, had not brought her here on false pretenses.

"Yes, I've decided it's definitely worthwhile. Even if I have to talk to the press," Pat said cheerfully.

The conference was held in one of the Parliament buildings. The Parliament Hill complex stood on a promontory above the Ottawa River like a huge Gothic symbol of justice.

The press was marvelously receptive to her. There was no cynical hostility to face, only predominantly grateful reporters who wanted to know every detail that was available about the proposed factory and the plane itself. Here, Pat met a hope that matched her own. Back home the Eagle was looked on as a whimsical invention that might never take flight—or as a possible threat to the already existing plane-manufacturing industry. Here the Eagle was looked on as a hopeful source of employment. The atmosphere was much more relaxed.

And again, Blaise sat at her side, lending his silent support.

As they left the reporters behind them, Pat glanced at her watch, knowing that they had to be at the Centre Block, which housed the House of Commons and the Senate, within half an hour. She was to meet five of the dignitaries in the Parliamentary Library, where everything could be settled informally—as informally as possible with a battery of lawyers looking on.

Pat wondered where they would meet their own legal council, who, Blaise had assured her, possessed outstanding credentials. Then a man waved to them, and she felt a resurgence of gratitude to Blaise for using his connections on her behalf. But a devil's advocate within her still wondered why he was going to such trouble.

"The press conference went very well," Blaise said as they crossed the threshold of the huge library.

Pat felt overwhelmed by the hushed, awe-inspiring atmosphere. The row of neatly attired men, all in their late fifties, rose in unison to greet her. "I guess I'm getting pretty good at press conferences," she whispered, drawing her courage around her like a protective cloak.

"That's not all you're getting good at," Blaise whispered back. A smile traced itself over Pat's lips and the row of men seemed to respond to it.

"Don't forget to be charming," Blaise advised, just before he made the appropriate introductions.

"I thought that was your department," she said between lips that hardly moved.

"It's your Eagle," he reminded her.

Yes. It was her Eagle. And she was relieved to hear him say that. So, he apparently thought that in the final analysis, she would have to do her own persuading.

And that was what she did. Armed with an endless supply of answers that had been embedded deep into her brain over the last year, Pat found herself equal to all the questions asked.

At first, they had been polite and simple. But Pat soon proved herself quite capable in the men's eyes. She noted that Blaise deliberately did not come to her rescue with answers when she paused. He let her pull herself out of her own traps. And this above all else compelled the men to look upon her seriously. Not that there was any question that they were all set, as representatives of their government, to pledge financial backing in exchange for the rights to the factory, but they had indicated at the beginning of the meeting that they believed themselves to be dealing with Blaise.

Pat had changed their minds and infected them with her enthusiasm as she spoke about the dream that was now hers.

"Gentlemen, we are on the threshold of something that could revolutionize air travel as we know it today. Ten years down the road, all the planes that are used will be built according to the specifications that are being laid down right now, and I do thank you for your vote of confidence and your farsightedness. For all inventions, once upon a time, were only dreams in the minds of their inventors. What the dreams need are men of faith and vision to make them a reality. And you are those men," Pat said as she beamed gratefully at them.

She sank back in her chair as the final arrangements were placed in the capable hands of the lawyers. She glanced at Blaise, who looked genuinely proud of her. "I told you she was something else," he said in an audible whisper to the government representatives.

A shared laugh signaled an end to business discussion and they adjourned to another room, where they enjoyed a sumptuous luncheon, away from the watchful eye of the press.

Pat could not believe it had truly happened. Thirty million dollars and a factory where they could produce the Eagle. All arranged within an hour. What sort of magician was this Blaise Hamilton? she wondered, stealing a glance at him over the rim of her wine glass.

"Do you really think you can have the 'bugs' out of your plane before January first?" a nattily dressed, wide-jowled senator asked Pat.

"Well, we certainly will try," Pat said with a smile. Then, after taking another sip, she looked into the man's catlike eyes. "Besides, we have no alternative," she said honestly. "We have to meet our deadline. The U.S. Cavalry always arrives in the nick of time."

Later that afternoon, when a session of the Senate was called, Pat and Blaise stayed and exchanged pleasantries with the five men who had become the saviors of her dream. During the whole period, whether she stood or sat, Pat felt that her knees were made entirely of water and she was amazed that they could support her at all. She hadn't realized how very frightened she was of the whole ordeal until it was over.

And she knew that she would never have made it without Blaise's support.

Ten

They stayed for a while, standing in the visitors' gallery overlooking the proceedings that went on on the Senate floor, just to get a touch of the local government. But in an hour's time they were back at their hotel.

"We could stay another day," Blaise said as Pat began to pack her suitcase. "I have the suite reserved until tomorrow night."

"No." Pat shook her head. "I'd better be getting back. There's so much to be done if we're to meet this deadline," she said, worrying that they could not.

"You haven't even seen your first Mountie," Blaise said. "How can you go back to New Mexico and tell them you didn't even see a Mountie?"

"I'll tell them they weren't in season," Pat said with a smile, neatly folding her cocktail dress. A flash of last night danced before her eyes as she did so.

"Mounties are always in season," Blaise said. "If you don't want to see Mounties, we could just stay here and see each other," he proposed, his voice growing warm and velvety as he took hold of both her hands.

That offer was much harder to cast aside. "Blaise," Pat said with effort, fighting her own longings. "I appreciate everything you've done for the project. . . ." Her voice trailed off.

"It wasn't all for the project," Blaise said. "Some of it was for me too," he said, running his fingers along her jawline. He turned her face up to his and kissed her, the kiss penetrating deep into her soul.

"Blaise, you're not making this easy," she said, her words struggling to be heard.

"Good," he replied. "I don't intend to make your escape from me easy. You've got your loan, you've got your backers, and a busy little crew working their hearts out for you," he said. "How about a little time for you and the white knight who came to your rescue?" he asked, tugging at her zipper, which began to slide down without much opposition from Pat.

"I've also got a family that's fighting me in court in a week and a deadline to meet," she reminded him, but her voice was far from firm as Blaise countinued undoing her clothes while his lips delivered soft, butterfly kisses on every inch of skin he uncovered.

"They'll keep," he promised. "And a few hours will make no difference to the deadline or the court."

She was about to give in to his powers of persuasion, when the phone rang, casting a shrill, cold hand over the pervading warmth.

"Damn Alexander Graham Bell's soul," Blaise muttered as he released her.

It was Sam.

"More trouble, boss lady," he said in his low-keyed voice, and it was as if a bucket of water had been thrown at Pat.

She gripped the phone with both hands. "What is it?" she asked tensely.

"Another part failed the stress test. Everything checked out okay, and then it just blew."

"Can it be replaced?" she asked.

"Sure, but it'll take time."

"We've got until the thirty-first of December to get it off the ground and tested under safety regulations," Pat reminded him, her nerves taut. Why was there always something?

There was a pause on the other end of the line, even though Sam knew about the deadline. "We can work in three shifts," he volunteered.

"Will they?" she asked.

Out of the corner of her eye, she watched Blaise pull out his own suitcase. He knew without a word obviously, that this put an end to any further lovemaking between them. At least for now.

"For you, boss lady, they'll probably jump through a few more hoops and do it gladly," Sam said.

"Well, someone isn't jumping through hoops for me," she said cryptically. "Do you suspect anyone?"

"Not a clue," he said, a trifle too quickly, Pat thought. "See you in the morning?"

"Yes. And, Sam—"

"Yes?"

"We've got thirty million dollars more to work with." She hoped that the news would make him feel better.

She knew Sam well enough to know that there would be no whoop of joy from him. Sam preferred to see life's limitations. "Let's hope we've got a plane to work with," he said and then hung up.

"Trouble?" Blaise asked as he finished his own packing and closed the lid on her suitcase.

Pat went to him, nodding absently. Had it been her imagination, or had Sam really answered her too quickly when she had asked if he suspected anyone? "Another failure."

"It'll all be ironed out in time," Blaise assured her.

"How do you do it?" she asked, turning to look at him. "How do you keep from worrying about details? You always seem so carefree."

"It won't help to worry. It dulls the senses. I try to keep one step ahead of it all. If that doesn't work, something else will," he said matter-of-factly. "Here," he said, tossing the box he had purchased yesterday on top of her suitcase.

Pat looked at him and then back at the box. So, it had been for her! With excited fingers, she opened it and found a long, cream-colored nightgown. The bodice was cut straight across, suspended on spaghetti straps and made of light lace. The sides fell straight down, with three straps of material lacing it together loosely on the side. Otherwise, it was completely slit up to the bodice. She held it up, then looked at Blaise with a question in her eyes.

"It's always sexier if there's a little something there to push aside," he said with a wicked look.

"I'm surprised someone's father or husband hasn't had you shot long ago," she said with a laugh, shaking her head as she gently folded the silky material. He had meant her to wear that tonight, with him. A pang came to her for a moment, thinking of what she was giving up. But there was still home, she thought, and Angelica slept soundly—or pretended to.

"I only prey on widows and orphans," he said with a wink. "Besides, you're not out of the woods yet, even if you're leaving this frosty climate. C'mon, Amelia Earhart, before we miss our flight and you blame that on me, too."

He wrapped her coat around her shoulders and picked up the two suitcases.

The flight home was much more pleasant and warm than the trip out had been. For the most part, her reservations about Blaise were gone. After all, Blaise had proven his respect for her, and besides, she was hopelessly in love with him. Except that now there was much more to it than losing her heart to a charismatic stranger across a crowded room. Now she appreciated the kind of man Blaise was.

Plus, he had managed to touch a part of her that she had never dreamed existed. He had changed her, opened her eyes to a wonderland that few knew of, and she could never be the same again. She would always love him for that, no matter what the future held.

As the plane landed, Blaise took her hand and

just held it. A vast wave of comfort came to Pat from that gesture as she looked into the warmth of his eyes. If only this could last, she thought sadly.

When they disembarked, they were engulfed by reporters and cameramen wanting to know if their "mission" had been as successful as rumored.

"New Mexican newspapers have precious little to write about," Pat said to Blaise over the din of questions.

"This isn't exactly in the same category as getting first prize in the taffy pull," Blaise replied, keeping her from minimizing her own accomplishments as he put a protective arm around her shoulders.

She liked that, too, she thought. No man had ever tried to bolster her morale. Roger had never tried to tear it down, that was true. But he hadn't shown the magnitude of his respect for her until just before he had died. Yes, Blaise was definitely one of a kind. No wonder no one had managed to snare him. He could get away with anything because of the way he made women feel while they were with him.

The reporters trailed them all the way to the car that Blaise had waiting for them. He truly had everything under control, she thought as they pulled away from the wall of reporters. And that, fortunately or unfortunately, included her too, she thought.

Angelica had a candlelit dinner waiting for them in the breakfast nook when they arrived.

"Also on your orders?" Pat asked as he helped her off with her coat.

"She's in your employ," he said innocently.

"Ah, but under your spell," Pat added wisely.

"And you?" he asked, handing her coat to Angelica, who then disappeared, leaving them alone in the intimately set kitchen. "Are you under my spell as well?" he asked, his face a scant inch above hers.

"If you have to ask," Pat said, her eyes dancing, "you're not as good a magician as I thought you were."

"Parrying and thrusting to the very end, eh?" Blaise asked glibly.

"For dear life," Pat answered as she slid into a chair. She looked down at the inviting dinner and found that she was much too tired to eat.

"Why?" Blaise asked, his eyes deep and searching as he sat down opposite her. His eyes never let go.

"Before you," Pat said carefully, trying to be honest, but avoiding his eyes, "Roger was the only other man in my life. I never saw myself as having a . . . relationship," she said, searching for a word that was delicate yet would not make Blaise think that she was trying to corner him. "Much less being part of a crowd of adoring women."

"You could never be part of a crowd," he said, not eating either as he studied her intently, his eyes warm and terribly inviting.

"Very gallant, Blaise," she said with a smile, wanting him to know she was no fool, despite her feelings for him.

"Very true, Patti," he said huskily.

"My turn," she said, raising her hand like a

schoolgirl. "Why did you 'ride to my rescue'?" she asked, curious as to what he would say.

"One," he said, ticking off the reasons on his fingers. "I thought I owed it to Roger. And two, I wanted to see how you really turned out. I'm not disappointed," he said, his eyes speaking volumes.

"You wouldn't say so if you were," she said, staring down at the swirl of cold mashed potatoes.

Blaise lifted her chin until her eyes met his. "I wouldn't be here if I were," he corrected. "Enough serious talk," he said, dismissing the subject with finality. "I've been patient long enough. I want to see what that nightgown looks like on a sensuous, mature, exciting woman."

"You do know how to turn a phrase," Pat said with a smile, trying to slow down her rapid heartbeat.

"I know how to *fit* a phrase," he said, already leading her to her bedroom.

Pat gave little thought to work that night, or to anything else, as paradise reached out to claim her. But the morning's light brought all the problems back to her and she was once more the chairman of the board, on whom the ultimate success or failure of the Eagle depended. She turned down Blaise's offer for both a ride to the plant and an early morning "pick-me-up," knowing that it would be far into the morning before she reached her destination if she gave in.

Sam was glad and grateful to see her. The same could not be said about Pardy, who complained about everything and bemoaned the fact that they would never be able to guarantee the success of the Eagle by the deadline. Pat took his words to heart, because he had been one of Roger's staunchest supporters in the early days and because she believed that Pardy knew what he was talking about. But somehow, somewhere along the line, Pardy had lost his enthusiasm.

"Do you think he's right?" Pat asked Sam when they were alone in her office that morning. Pardy had left them reluctantly, apparently not liking the fact that Pat turned to Sam rather than him for advice.

Sam leaned his long frame against the doorjamb, looking at the retreating back of the foreman. "Logically, he probably has something there. The men have been working awfully hard on something that, well, could just be a pipe dream. Despite the shares, there's only so long you can work on faith and hope."

"That's just it," Pat cried. "Faith and hope. Sam, we don't have anything else. Oh, I know we've got those bright, quick-witted engineers out of Cal Tech and M.I.T., but without the enthusiasm, without the will, well, this thing could be years away from completion." Pat sighed, shoving her hands into her deep pockets.

"That's why I wanted you back," Sam said. "You're that enthusiasm, that spark that keeps them going. We both know that you don't know all that much about what's happening here—oh, enough to get us the right publicity," he added positively, "but not enough to handle any actual problems. But it's your belief in the men's capabilities, belief in Mr. Hamilton's designs and vision that fuels the others to keep on trying when every test goes haywire."

Pat's smile was deep and grateful as she said, "Sam, I've known you for fifteen years and that's the most I have ever heard out of your mouth at one clip."

"That's the most you've heard out of my mouth in a month," Sam corrected solemnly, "but when a thing needs saying, I'll say it."

Pat smiled at him fondly. "Well, I'd better go into the ranks, then, and spread some enthusiasm. We need instant goodwill if we're to finish. Where's our main problem?" she asked as they left the office together, heading for the ground floor and the assembly line.

With Sam's words ringing in her ears, Pat felt compelled to spend more time in the office and turned down several of Blaise's offers for lunch and dinner. She wondered, when she got the chance, what Blaise was doing to keep himself occupied and found that thoughts in that direction only distressed and distracted her from her job.

Sam was right. She didn't know all that much, although she knew oceans more than she had a year ago. But her encouraging words, her willingness to listen, whether to a job-related problem or perhaps a few words of complaint about home life, endeared Pat to each and every one of the people who worked for her.

That was why it was so difficult for her to accept the idea that someone within the network was against her. A sabotage of the engine had been attempted. Someone who knew the operation had done it or had it done. It hurt.

·   ·   ·

Pat's involvement with work helped her push aside some of the tension of waiting for the trial. Blaise had once again come to her aid, supplying her with the able assistance of Blair Afton, the lawyer who had helped draw up the agreement in Ottawa. Her own lawyer was disgruntled when he was pushed aside. But once his wounded pride was healed, the man was relieved to be out of Mother Rose's line of fire.

Pat would gladly have run for cover herself that overcast, brisk Friday morning in the beginning of December as she watched the members of Roger's family file in, keeping Sara and Bucky within their ranks. On her side of the court sat Aunt Delia in her wheelchair, daring the young deputy to instruct her to take a seat and allow the wheelchair to be pushed out of the way. The tall, blond, gawky young man looked at Delia once or twice and apparently decided that it was in his best interests to steer clear of the matter. That brought the only smile to Pat's face that morning, covering the ache she felt at having her own children visibly side with Mother Rose and the others against her. Blaise sat directly behind her and left only when Jonathan and Allen entered the court.

To Pat's overwhelming surprise, the two hailed him, and he worked his way to the back of the room. After a rather lengthy conversation with them, he reseated himself behind Pat.

She looked at him quizzically, but Blaise offered her no words. As she turned toward the front of the court, the deputy called for all to rise.

Pat wondered what Roger's brothers had said to Blaise. They had probably been trying to draw

him into their conspiracy, but she knew now that
they could never succeed. But why had the conversation taken so long? And why was Blaise re-
luctant to talk about it? She barely heard the
instructions to sit, and Blair gave her sleeve a
slight tug. She turned to look at Blaise and he
offered her a confident high sign. Her emotions
churned within her. Why was nothing simple?
Why was nothing cut-and-dried? Oh, Roger, why
did you have to die and do this to me? she thought
almost in desperation before a calm came over
her. No, no one was forcing her to do this. It was
her fight now, and fight she would. If either Jonathan or Mother Rose or anyone else thought they
could wrest control of Hamilton Enterprises from
her, they had another think coming.

She looked up at the middle-aged judge with a
new light of determination in her eyes. Let them
all do their damnedest—she'd meet them head
on!

The trial was rather a disappointment for the
press, Pat later realized. They would have preferred
that it drag on for days, possibly months, but it
was over in short order. The judge was, as it
turned out, sympathetic to Pat, who, with only two
people in her corner, was obviously the underdog.

The winning stroke was both Roger's physician,
who gave testimony that he could not see where
any of Roger's mental faculties were impaired,
and the agreement that Pat had obtained from
the Canadian government for thirty million dollars.

"If I were to rule that Mrs. Hamilton is lacking

in judgment for carrying out her late husband's wishes, I would also be accusing members of the Canadian government of the same thing, and I for one would not want to start an international incident over this. Who am I to call members of the House of Commons and the Prime Minister himself a fool?" he asked, his white hair shaking vigorously as he made his statement. "That sort of criticism," he added solemnly, "I reserve for members of our own Senate in the privacy of my own home."

The spectators ate it up.

Pat joyfully shook the young lawyer's hand, clutching it with relief. This part of the ordeal was over. Her public heartache was at an end, she thought. But as she turned to say something to Blaise, she found only Delia behind her. Looking around, Pat spied Blaise leaving the court with Jonathan. What was going on?

"Well, you've done it!" Delia said, her voice cackling with glee. "You knocked the pants off Rose. It'll take her some time to climb back up on her tuffet this time," she said, her thin lips spreading widely in a grin.

Pat only half heard her.

It was a quiet celebration at Pat's house, just Delia and the lawyer and Pat. Blaise was conspicuously absent. What was he doing? she wondered. Had he been with Jonathan all this time? More than anything, she wanted him here to share her moment of triumph.

"Out with it, Pat," Delia said in her no-nonsense

voice. "You don't look like someone who's just won a big case. What's on your mind?"

Blair Afton took this as his cue to leave, after offering Pat wishes for continued success with the Eagle.

Pat paced around, feeling slightly freer now that she was alone with her aunt. Delia had been like a second mother to her in the early years of her marriage, and she had always valued Delia's judgment and support. But this was no easy matter to relate. After all, Delia doted on Blaise.

"It's Blaise," Pat said finally.

"I thought it might be," Delia said, nodding knowingly. "That boy makes me wish I weren't his relative and that I was some twenty years younger," she said with a cackle.

Her words made Pat smile. "Only twenty?" she asked.

Delia nodded. "He likes older women."

Pat stared out at the white gazebo in her garden and watched as the afternoon sun retreated from it, leaving it in shadow. "I hadn't noticed."

"Oh, hadn't you?" Delia asked wisely. Her tone indicated that she did not believe Pat.

Pat turned around. "It's not what you think," she said, looking fondly at the leathery, wrinkled old face with its sunken cheeks. Delia had gone through a lot in her day and she hated to make her suffer. Her mind searched for a way to retreat verbally.

"I might be old, Pat, but I'm not an old fool. I can still see. You perk up like a schoolgirl every time he comes into the room. And him, he's a proud one, that boy. He knows what he looks like, knows what the ladies think when they see him—"

"Yes, I know," Pat murmured in a voice that was tinged with sadness.

"—but I've only seen that special light in his eyes when he looks at you once before," Delia concluded, not letting Pat interrupt.

Pat suddenly came to attention. "What?" she asked. "When?"

"He had it that time I found the two of you out on the terrace the night of your engagement party," Delia said, nodding knowingly.

"He's seen a lot of women since then, most of them away from your eyes," Pat said patiently, not allowing herself to take any stock in what Delia was telling her. She wouldn't have her hopes raised just to have them dashed to pieces in the end.

Delia shrugged. "He hasn't been married once, has he?" she pointed out, peering at Pat's face.

"He's probably having too much fun to say 'I do.'" Pat countered.

Delia shook her head. "Have it your way. But someday," she said, wagging a bony finger at her, "you'll stop and see I was right."

Pat merely smiled at the old woman, thinking how many other old people said things like that every day, hoping to have events bear them out. But no, not this time. Blaise Hamilton was too much the worldly gentleman, too much the ladies' man. He had everything to lose and nothing to gain by losing his heart to one Patrissa Hamilton— if he even had a heart to lose, which she was beginning to doubt.

Delia was right on one score, though. Blaise had not been married, never even engaged as far as she knew. That seemed rather odd for a man of his age and with his vast appeal to women—and his vast talents around women. She would have bet that more than one woman had tried in earnest to snare him. Perhaps his love, his real love, was wheeling and dealing. He did seem to thrive on it.

Perhaps Blaise really had no heart to give.

So why did her own ache so at the very thought?

Eleven

Blaise did not return until very, very late that night. Although Pat had become a rather direct person in the past year, she was too afraid to confront him with her feelings. An outright rejection would ruin her, she felt, and there was a lot of work to be done.

She went to the office early Saturday morning and stayed there, doing what she could, burying herself in reports and the slow process of rectifying each error that rose its menacing head within the body of the Eagle.

"When I said your presence added to the workers' enthusiasm for the project, I didn't mean for you to sleep with the drawing board and the components," Sam said on Sunday morning, when he discovered her at her desk.

Pat looked up at him with tired eyes. She had spent the night on the couch, not wanting to go home. Silly, wasn't it? A grown woman hiding out. Blaise, though, did not seem even to care that she was missing. He hadn't called the office, hadn't come. With the prospect of victory so close at hand, she felt strangely hollow inside. When she had called home late last night, it was Angelica who had answered, not a worried Blaise. He was probably sleeping peacefully in some woman's arms, she thought ruefully. What a fool she was for aching this way. When Angelica arrived with her change of clothing, she was going to pull herself together and show Blaise Hamilton that although she was grateful for any so-called help he had given her, her life did not begin and end in his arms. Even though it did.

"I thought I should give my undivided attention to this," Pat lied, pointing to the latest report that had crossed her desk.

Sam nodded, but she could see that he didn't believe her. "What you need is a little diversion," he said. "My people are having their annual Shalako ceremony next weekend. Why don't you go see it? You said you enjoyed yourself the last time."

The last time had been just after Roger had died and Sam had taken her to get her mind away from that. Preparations for the feast took some forty-nine days, and the departure of the Shalako, or giant messengers of the rain gods, signaled an end to a season. Somehow, it seemed fitting. She looked up at Sam and nodded.

"Okay, we'll see."

Sam did not press her any further, leaving Pat to stare at the reports and hope that Angelica would come soon. She knew that beneath her white lab coat she was a rumpled mess—at least that was the way she felt.

Within a few minutes the door opened again. Strange that Angelica would come in without knocking, Pat thought as she turned her swivel chair away from the window and toward the door, fully expecting to see her housekeeper carrying the clothes she had requested.

"I thought it was about time you stopped hiding out and came home."

Pat was startled to hear Blaise's deep voice. One look at him showed her that he had lost no sleep over anything. He looked well and rested—perfect, as always. He even sported that ever-present mischievous glint in his eye. Well, this time it wasn't going to work!

"I have a lot of work to do," she said, her mouth drawing back tightly.

"All work and no play . . ." Blaise began, then let his voice trail off as he stood back and studied her.

He could see right through her, she knew, and it annoyed her desperately. "I've been playing much too much of late," she said sharply, pretending to read a report.

Blaise came around, putting himself between her and her desk, blocking out the report and anything else that was there. "And it's been wonderful—or have I suddenly turned into a poor judge of character?" he asked.

"I don't know about you, but I certainly have," she said, drawing on inner courage that she didn't think she had. She had to confront him with her anger. She had to.

"What's on your mind, Patti?" he asked in a

voice that was tender and low. His eyes spoke to her, saying soft things that she couldn't bear to feel right now.

"Don't call me Patti," she snapped, trying to cut into the power he seemed to have over her.

"All right, Mrs. Hamilton," he said, crossing his arms in front of him, "although it's a little silly to revert back to that state since I'm probably one of the few people, besides your doctor, who knows where your birthmark is," he concluded, his eyes dancing. "But all right, all right," he said hurriedly, holding up his hands to fend off her words. "What's bothering you?"

"You are!" she snapped, getting up and walking away from him.

He seemed to consider that for a moment. "That's never been a problem before," he said wickedly.

"Your insensitivity is," she said angrily. Why did he disarm her at every turn? her soul cried.

He did not lose his good humor, although his eyes grew a little darker as they narrowed. "What are you talking about?"

"You know very well what I'm talking about!"

"I need more of a hint than that, Mrs. Hamilton. If I knew what you were talking about, I wouldn't be asking. Now in plain English, without any code words—out with it!" he commanded, and she saw how he could take charge of a large assembly or any situation he found himself in. There was something dynamically compelling about him, even as the cloud of pain around her threatened to burst.

"Blaise, where did you go after the trial?" she queried, desperately fighting the impulse to melt into his arms. But she knew that this inevitable confrontation would be even more difficult in the future if she pushed her anger aside.

His expression was placid, though Pat noticed his eyes deepen from cerulean blue to cool violet. "I was with the Hamiltons. You saw me leave with Jonathan and Allen." Not impish or tender now, his soft tone sent a chill through Pat's heart. She forced herself to press on.

"You said you didn't get along with them."

"I don't," he said, his eyes watching her every movement. "They're a bunch of snobbish, insensitive, air-headed, empty-hearted people."

"So what on earth were you talking to them about?" she demanded. "And why didn't you say anything about where you were going?" Pat gathered up every ounce of courage in her being and plunged forward. "I hope you remember that there is more between us than there is between most business acquaintances. I wanted to share the joy and relief of winning the court battle with you. Clearly, you find the company of a bunch of snobbish and empty-hearted and whatever-else people preferable to mine. I'm not even worth a phone call in your estimation. Now you can't seem to figure out why I'm upset. Well, I'm beginning to think that you are everything the rest of the Hamiltons are." She concluded with a great deal more bitterness than she had intended.

Understanding and sympathy emanated from Blaise as he leaned ever so slightly toward her. "You might have given me an opportunity to explain before you started playing hide-and-go-seek."

"I'm giving you one now," she said, swallowing hard.

"Jonathan tried to buy me," he said simply.

"Just as I thought," she replied, waiting.

"I tried to talk him and Aunt Rose into pulling out gracefully and not contesting the decision. I tried to talk them into either backing you or at least healing the rift. I knew how much it bothered you to be the Lone Ranger in this setup. I hated every minute I spent talking to those people. I've dealt with friendlier enemies of the government in my time. The worst-mannered nomad is at bottom kinder than they are. You have no need of them in your life anymore.

"And I'm sorry about not telling you where I was. Jonathan cornered me right after the trial, and our discussion absorbed me so thoroughly, I wasn't even aware of how much time had gone by."

Pat felt terrible. She had let her anger fester and grow out of proportion while Blaise once again had donned his armor and fought on her behalf. "Blaise?" she said, feeling embarrassed.

"Yes?"

"I have been rash, and I'm sorry."

"You should be," he said, but this time there was a tiny hint of a smile in his voice.

"Will you stay?" she asked.

"No."

Her heart dropped. She deserved this. The only man who had come to her aid and bucked everything to help her and she hadn't trusted him.

"But you can come with me," he added. "I'm only going back to the house." His eyes were shining again. "My bed's gotten cold."

"Why, you . . . !" But her voice trailed off as a lightness came back to her soul. The tightness in her chest was gone.

"Even God rested on Sunday, and He had a little more to take care of than the Eagle," Blaise said, taking her hand.

Pat offered no protest as she went with him.

"Have you stayed here the entire time?" he asked as they went to his car. She nodded. "Okay, I'll help you shower," he promised.

A tingle went through Pat's body at the promise of things to come.

Pat took Sam up on his offer. The Eagle was still very, very important to her, but she realized now that undoubtedly, upon its completion, Blaise would move on to something else. She tried to put her sadness aside and enjoy their remaining days together. She wouldn't repeat Roger's mistake. He had lived his life entirely at the plant, and had missed out on much of life's beauty. Well, after Blaise left, there would be all the time in the world to be in her office.

They took the weekend off and drove through the desert, armed with Sam's directions. They looked in awe at nature's handiwork, such as Venus's Needle, stretching up toward the sky northwest of Gallup. The temperature that day was brisk but not cold, certainly not the way it had been in Ottawa. As they drove to the Zuni Pueblo, Pat thought how much she would have liked to be on a bearskin rug somewhere, stretched out by a warm cabin fire, with only Blaise to take the chill from her body. Someday, she thought— but she knew that someday would not be. This was all she had, the present.

The festival at the Zuni Pueblo was spectacular,

and Pat and Blaise lost themselves, pretending to be tourists and enjoying all the "firsts" that native dwellers always seem to miss. The ceremonies began that evening at sundown, when the messengers of the rain gods were received and conducted through the new homes that were dedicated to them. The dancing and feasting that were held in honor of the Shalako continued through the night and into the next evening, when the ceremony was over and the Pueblo was closed to visitors until after the winter solstice.

The swirling colors of the Zunis' costumes made Pat think of the colors that emerged in her head each time Blaise made love to her, and the smile she wore through the ceremonial dancing was not lost on him.

Nothing was lost on Blaise. He seemed to be everywhere in the next few days, supporting her both at work and at home, where he arrived before her and had candlelit dinners waiting. These were followed by nights of ecstasy. Despite the rift with her children, despite the fantastic pressures at work in trying to meet the deadline, Pat had never been happier in her life.

Time slipped away, and suddenly it was only a week from the deadline and they were far from prepared. Many of the employees had given up their Christmas, a time when the plant was normally closed, to work around the clock on the Eagle. But Blaise had insisted, as had Sam, that Pat spend Christmas Eve at home with a few friends.

"You've been driving yourself relentlessly," Blaise said, picking Pat up early at work and bringing her home, "and you look tired."

"Could be due to the fact that I'm not getting any sleep at night," she said with a smile.

"Complaining?" he asked, glancing at her as he made his way past the huge black gates and down the long, winding driveway. Luis was away visiting relatives, on Pat's insistence.

"Bragging," she replied, nestling closer against him as she wrapped her arm through the crook in his right elbow. Oh, this would end all too soon, she thought as a deep pang came into her heart. She pushed the thought away with force. Not now, she mustn't spoil this evening with sad thoughts.

Angelica had everything ready by the time they arrived, and Delia sat in the corner, opposite the nine-foot Christmas tree that stood behind the long sofa and juxtaposed loveseat. The old woman was issuing orders to a tired-looking Angelica, who brought out a tray of eggnog as soon as Pat entered.

Pat laughed. "I don't think I need all this to get me in a holiday mood," she said, taking a glass as Angelica set the tray down.

Blaise looked at Delia, who nodded. Pat caught the exchange and wondered what was going on, but had no time to phrase her question.

"No," Blaise said, "but I think you might like this," he said, guiding her to her bedroom.

"Blaise, not now," she hissed, very conscious of the fact that Delia was watching them with a broad smile on her thin lips.

"I couldn't wrap your present," Blaise was saying, not paying any attention to her protests, "but I didn't think you'd mind." He opened the door to her room and turned her face toward it, keeping back any words of protest. Pat opened her eyes wide as tears came to them.

"Hello, Mother."

"Merry Christmas, Mom."

Pat's arms flew around her two children as Sara and Bucky almost contritely joined her.

"How . . . ? Why . . . ?" She looked at Blaise, who was obviously enjoying the reunion.

"Stutters a lot, doesn't she?" he said to the two younger people, ushering the tall, blond youngster and his sister out of the bedroom. He looked back amiably at Pat. "This was why I spent so much time with old Jonathan. Actually, it takes very little time to say 'go to hell.' But convincing these two of the dream that you have took a bit longer. I got them to see it your way without alienating Aunt Rose—although that wouldn't be the worst thing in the world," he said to Pat as they went back to the living room.

Guests had begun to arrive and it was several minutes before Pat found herself with Blaise again, having to play the good hostess and also make sure that her children were well provided for.

"I don't know how you do it," Pat said, sharing a glass of eggnog with Blaise as they stood off to the side of the long holiday-draped table and watched people mingle.

"I told you, I'm a genius," Blaise said easily, his eyes lazily glancing over her, making her warm.

"Now if you could only tell me who's responsible for those accidents and that break-in at work . . ."

"Well, I do have my suspicions about your inside 'rat.' "

"Who?" Pat asked, her eyes wide open.

But Blaise shook his head. "Uh-uh. This is a

Christmas party. There'll be no more shop talk now. I'll tell you once I'm sure," he said, as he began maneuvering her to the left.

"What are you doing?" she asked as she saw him grin.

"Mistletoe," he said, pointing upward. And in front of Sara and Bucky, Blaise kissed her. No one seemed to disapprove.

Pat stayed up late that night, talking with her children, catching up on everything. She found that they had plans for the day after Christmas and could stay with her only until then. But they were together almost constantly. During that time, Pat got sufficient additional insight into her late husband's family to dislike them forever.

"Uncle Jonathan had us convinced you were a raving loony," Bucky said flatly as they sat in the kitchen the morning of their departure.

"You might have remembered what I was like," Pat pointed out gently.

"What we remembered," Sara said, "was how devoted you were to Dad. How dinners were rescheduled for him and trips were cut short on his orders because he had to be back to take care of some detail or other. You always gave in to Dad— and he wasn't always the most practical of men. And he did have inventions that failed miserably," Sara concluded, putting down her coffee cup.

Pat knew that this was Jonathan speaking because Sara was too young to recall those things on her own. But she agreed. "He did that."

"So, when Uncle Jonathan and Grandmother Rose pointed out that Dad's mind was failing and he was giving away pieces of the company, pieces that belonged to us," Bucky said matter-of-factly

as he made himself another sandwich, "we believed him."

"And Uncle Jonathan said that you were under
his thumb with that deathbed promise to make a
paper airplane," Sara chimed in.

"What changed your minds?" Pat asked, toying
with her food as they sat in the sun-splattered
kitchen. She was due at the office an hour ago
but could not tear herself away from Sara and
Bucky.

"Blaise," Sara told her. "He pointed out that it
took a lot of guts on your part to go against everyone, and that a weak person who was pliable
would have thrown in the towel a thousand fail-
ures ago. And then he threw a lot of technical
stuff at us to explain why Dad's plane could really
fly."

"He told us we had a genius for a father," Bucky
continued, "and that while some of his inventions
hadn't worked, most of them had. He also said
that in giving away pieces of the company, Dad
was insuring that the top-notch crew he had as-
sembled would stay with the project after he was
gone."

"In a way," Sara said, her eyes dropping a little,
"he made us ashamed of ourselves, putting money
in place of the loyalty we should have given you. I
guess there's a lot of Uncle Jonathan in us," Sara
said.

Pat put her arm around her daughter for a
moment, giving her a quick hug. "There's a lot of
your father in there too. Don't you doubt it for a
second," she said fiercely. "And it's all over. We're
a family again. Nothing can stop us now," Pat
said with enthusiasm.

Just as Pat was leaving, Sara stopped her. "I won't be here when you get back," Sara said in the doorway of her old room, "but I just wanted you to know something."

"What?" Pat asked, cocking her head.

"I think you're pretty terrific," the girl blurted out, then disappeared from view.

Pat was humming as she went out to the car. A newly arrived Luis stood patiently waiting on the driver's side. As she slid in, Pat found Blaise sitting in the back.

"Hi," he said as casually as if they were meeting for a date.

Impulsively, Pat leaned over and kissed him in gratitude for bringing her children back to her.

"Well, I must remember to say 'hi' more often," Blaise said just before he drew her into his arms and kissed her soundly. "God, that feels good. This behaving for the children was beginning to get to me. Are they still leaving?" he asked.

She nodded. "This afternoon."

"Good," he pronounced with a smile. "My celibacy can only last so long," he said, looking at his watch. "And there's only five hours left—if you don't meet me in a local motel for 'lunch,' I might do something desperate."

Pat began to laugh and it was a long, rich laugh. She laughed until her sides ached. She laughed from happiness and from her joy in life. "Blaise," she said, trying to catch her breath, "you're wonderful."

"Absolutely no argument there," he said as he closed the little curtain that separated Luis from the backseat and drew a tiny, private world around them.

"What are you doing?" Pat asked, her voice playful.

"I intend to do as much damage as is humanly possible in the next twenty-three miles," he said just before his hands began to undo the buttons on the front of her dress.

Twelve

All that Blaise's kisses and caresses managed to do was unsettle Pat terribly for the task that lay at hand. By the time Luis had pulled into her customary parking place, her clothing was back in place, but her heart was beating hard and her desire had mounted greatly, absolutely unquenched.

"Always leave them wanting more," Blaise murmured into her ear as he helped her out of the car.

She knew it would be useless to hold her head high and pretend that she was unaffected. He had grown to know her far too well for that. Besides, it felt wonderful not to have to act anymore. The only acting that would be required was the performance she would give when he finally left her side. Then it would be a struggle not to cry out and ask him to stay. But she knew that if she did,

164

she would cast a pall on all that had gone on between them. Blaise Hamilton needed no clinging vines, and until he had come into her life, she had not thought of herself in that light. But oh, how she wished she could cling to him until all eternity melted into an abyss and left her with her lover.

Five days were all they had left before the major tests. Five days of constant work and agony. Part of her wanted to be alone with Blaise at all times, but there was too much responsibility on her shoulders to give in to that temptation. And Blaise seemed to understand it all, which made him that much more precious to her.

Sara called twice to wish her well and to make her apologies for not being able to be there "on the big day." As it drew nearer, Pat began really to fear that it would not come into being at all, and then all their work would be for nothing.

To allow themselves a safety margin, Sam and Pat had decided on an actual test flight to be done on December 30th. That way, they had room for error. And error they had.

As they stood in the desert, waiting for the test pilot, one swaggering Monty O'Toole, to take the Eagle up and make her soar, Pat gripped Blaise's hand so tightly that she suddenly realized her nails were digging into his flesh. But he kept on holding it, giving it a comforting squeeze.

The plane sputtered and they heard the jet engine whine, straining to make contact. With a crew of twenty-five standing around in a wide U at the rear, the plane moved several feet, then stopped, unable to continue.

Pat looked at Pardy, her heart in her mouth.

"What is it?" she asked, feeling as if her mouth had cotton in it.

He shrugged, looking somewhat disgusted. "The electrical system."

Pat turned to Blaise, searching for some magic, comforting word, and saw that he was not looking at either her or the plane. He was looking at Pardy.

"How can you tell?" Blaise challenged.

Pardy stopped in his tracks, scowling at Blaise. His retort was directed at Pat. "Look, I've got better things to do than talk to all these people you keep pulling in as 'advisers,' Mrs. Hamilton." He turned on his heel, about to go back to the Eagle.

"I don't think so," Blaise said, putting himself in front of the man and stopping his departure. Blaise stood a good five inches taller than Pardy, and although the foreman was younger, Blaise was in much better shape physically. "Sam," Blaise called to the Indian, who had watched the exchange silently, "could you tell that it was the electrical system just by listening?" he asked casually.

"Nope."

Blaise's eyes seemed to bore into Pardy. "So what makes you so sure it's the electrical system?" he asked smoothly, his voice deadly calm.

Pardy squirmed. "I'm not sure. It's just a lucky guess," he snapped nervously.

Pat stared at the two men, bewildered. She had known Pardy for so many years. . . .

Behind them, her crew was running to check out the problem as a disgruntled O'Toole stepped out of the cockpit. But the drama before Pat was far more intense.

"I think it's more than a lucky guess," Blaise said to the foreman. "I think you know something."

"You're crazy!" Pardy shouted, obviously anxious to get away from the whole scene.

"Sam," Pat said quietly, her eyes never leaving Pardy, "see what Dale says," she said, referring to the head engineer.

The answer came back a few minutes later. "He's not sure, but he suspects a problem with the electrical system," Sam said. All eyes were now on Pardy.

Blaise grabbed the shorter man by the collar. "And you're going to tell him just what that problem is, aren't you?" he asked.

Pardy refused to answer until a yelp of pain escaped his lips as Blaise twisted his arm behind his back.

"Aren't you?" Blaise asked again, his voice still sounding pleasant to the untrained ear.

Pat felt shattered and angrier than she had been in a long time as she addressed the foreman. "So it was you all along," she said, her voice bitter. How could she have neglected to notice the hostility that she saw in Pardy's eyes? "Why in heaven's name did you do it?" she demanded. "You were Roger's right-hand man. I trusted you!"

" 'Were,' " Pardy repeated, his lip curling in disgust. "Until that Indian came into the picture. Then all of a sudden, an ex-con's advice was taken in the same light as mine." His small eyes looked at her darkly.

"That's still no reason to do this to the Eagle!" Pat said hotly.

"Maybe fifty thousand dollars is, though," Blaise said, pushing Pardy toward the car that he and the others had arrived in.

"Fifty thousand dollars?" Pat echoed, waiting for an explanation.

"That was what Jonathan promised to pay him," Blaise said, motioning Pardy into the backseat.

"Jonathan told you that?" Pat asked incredulously.

"Jonathan wouldn't admit to his own name upon direct questioning," Blaise said, sitting down beside Pardy as Pat got in the front seat next to Sam. "But when he asked me to help him, he alluded to the fact that I wouldn't have to do any of the dirty work—that there was already someone there who was capable of doing plenty. He just wanted me along for insurance."

"What made you suspect Wade?" she asked, looking at the foreman contemptuously. Pardy lowered his eyes, which glowed like red coals of anger.

"Sam saw him skulking around after the break-in. He wasn't really supposed to be there that day, but made up some story that he was worried about the project and didn't trust the security men I had hired. Sam felt that if he accused him, the accusation would be discarded because of the situation between these two and because Pardy had seniority. So he told me," Blaise concluded, as if that said it all.

Pat turned to look at Sam, who looked forward impassively as he guided the car back to the plant. "My God, you've even got Sam in your corner. Is there anything you can't do?" she asked, turning back to Blaise.

"I can't think of one thing," he said and let the matter drop there.

Pat turned back around, not saying anything.

• • •

The Eagle was brought back, and with Pardy's admission of what he had done, the crew at least knew what they were up against. They worked until the wee hours of the morning, trying to rectify the problem, but it wasn't until two the next afternoon, the afternoon of their deadline, that the plane was once more perched on the runway in the desert, waiting for its maiden voyage.

O'Toole wore his lucky scarf jauntily around his neck as he climbed in again, his fingers crossed and held aloft.

"I think he sees himself as the Red Baron," Blaise muttered. "But, whatever works . . ." He and Pat were standing in the same spot they had been in the day before.

Pat was rigid with tension as she witnessed the Eagle's growing success. It went through its low-speed tests without a single problem. Thank God they had managed to fix the electrical system in time, she thought with relief, shading her eyes from the bright winter sun. Her spirits began to soar as high as she hoped the plane would go. One after another, the tests were passed satisfactorily as the government official at her elbow checked off a list he held on a clipboard. Thomas Blakely, the man representing the Canadian government, stood next to him, his face just as mesmerized as Pat's was.

The high-speed tests were gone through in haste, as if the pilot was afraid if they dallied, they would not make it. Suddenly Pat saw smoke coming from the brake area.

"They're overheating!" she cried to Blaise, pointing. She noted that Blaise looked a little worried himself, and panic gripped her heart. Blaise had never looked worried before.

Oh, please let them hold, she thought. Just let them hold until the test is over. Only one more to go, she prayed, looking at the government official's list.

On the last test, the high-speed taxi test, one of the brakes almost exploded. Sparks flew, and a tire went up in flames. Then another blew, and another, and another.

Pat stood on the edge of the runway, numb. The plane had no wheels and was engulfed in a cloud of black smoke as several people ran around it with fire extinguishers. As the fire went out, so did Pat's spirits.

"It's over," she said in a voice that was devoid of emotion. She was so drained, she was surprised that she was standing up at all. "All those hours of work, over, in one cloud of smoke. Gone. Vanished." She sighed deeply, not even seeing the expression on Blakely's face.

She was aware of the fact that it was Sam who took her home, not Blaise. Blaise did not come home until several hours after that, and by then Pat had gone to bed, refusing Angelica's offer of dinner, turning down the invitation she had gotten earlier to attend a New Year's Eve party. There was nothing to celebrate anymore. It was all over. Done. Tomorrow need not come, she thought as she pulled the covers over her head, trying hard to shut out all thoughts.

A sleepless eternity later, Pat felt a light tug on her blanket.

"Is this a private party, or can anyone join in?" Blaise asked.

Her arm felt as if it weighed a thousand pounds as she went to pull back the blanket. But Blaise beat her to it. The smile on his face was endearing, and for a moment she forgot her depression.

"I thought only little girls pulled the covers over their heads when they try to pretend the world isn't there."

"I wish I were a little girl," Pat said heavily, lying against her sky-blue pillow. "Then I wouldn't be involved in any of this."

"Ah, but then I'd be hauled away on charges of contributing to the delinquency of a minor," he said.

He succeeded in making her smile. "Well, that's the first step," he said, sitting down next to her and putting his feet up on the bed. "Now that we've established the fact that you are back among the living and are smiling—sort of—let's find out what else you can do. Besides cry," he said, tracing the path where her tears had dried. His touch was so very gentle, she thought.

But she shook her head. "All those people were depending on me," she said, her voice echoing hollowly in her head.

"You're not the one who blew a tire," he said gently.

"I might as well have been," she said dejectedly. "All I can keep thinking is—now what?"

"Well, tomorrow's 'now what' will be taking that last test again with new tires," Blaise began.

"What for?" she said hopelessly.

"Patti, it's not like you to give up so easily. The Eagle is nearly ready to fly, and there are other resources for funding we can explore. It's only money, remember?"

Pat appreciated his effort to cheer her, but she could not eliminate the overwhelming sense of disappointment that permeated her soul.

"And as for what happens next, I have a pretty good suggestion." He turned onto his side to look at her.

"I don't feel like going to a party," she said, thinking that he was referring to the invitation she had turned down. It had included both of them.

"How about a private one?" he asked. "I promise not to bring even one noise maker." He kissed her bare arm lightly.

In a single act, he ignited her soul, which needed more than passion tonight. Tonight she needed to be held and loved and assured that all would be well. She needed to have someone make her forget about tomorrow and all the other tomorrows that would carry disappointments with them.

If anyone could accomplish that, Blaise could.

Blaise did.

He took her in his arms and kissed the traces of her tears away softly. His lips brushed hers gently and lovingly at first. He stroked her over and over again, comforting tenderness changing into a passionate tide of motion meant to arouse her very being, which it did all too quickly.

Pat felt herself shedding the mourning pall that had taken hold of her and lifted her arms up to him, putting them around his neck. Her fingers entwined themselves in his thick hair, pulling him toward her. Blaise had managed to wiggle her out of her nightgown. His kisses replaced the straps on her shoulders and found their way down to her heaving breasts. His tongue slowly encircled her hardening nipples, making them peak beneath his mouth as she arched her back up against him, yearning to feel his hot body against her own, drawing comfort, strength, and passion from it.

The spell he wove around her grew as all disappointments were magically pushed from her mind. Nothing mattered now except for Blaise and their private world of fire. She felt her heart pounding as he took her once and then again, a blanketing feeling of peace mingling with new surging desire. All her fears melted in the heat of his kisses as his mouth scorched her skin, laying claim to every inch of her. She moaned in pleasure and anticipation as she sank deeper into the silken sheets. Her mouth clung hungrily to his as satisfaction smothered her senses and paradise drifted back into the mists from which it had come.

"Feeling better?" he asked, looking down at her with a soft, sweet expression.

She opened her eyes to look at him. He was propped up on one elbow, smiling. The look on his face was kinder than any she had ever seen on him. It was devoid of any teasing, any mischief.

"You could make hell bearable," she said, a dreamy expression on her face.

"That, Patti, is the nicest thing you've ever said to me," he said, playfully tugging back the sheet that she had wrapped around her breasts.

"You should have nice things said to you," she said, lovingly touching his face, totally disregarding his pulling at the sheet. She held his face against the palm of her hand. "You're a thoroughly nice person."

"That's not what you thought a little while ago," he reminded her humorously.

"I was a paranoid woman fighting a multiheaded dragon and trying to fly a paper plane," she said with a sigh.

"It'll fly," he assured her.

"One day too late," she replied bitterly.

Blaise said nothing.

"Well, at least it brought us together for a while," she said, and wondered why he looked at her so curiously when she said those words. "I'll always be grateful for that."

The clock in the hall chimed twelve times. Blaise lifted her chin until her lips offered themselves to him. "Happy New Year, Patti, darling," he said, kissing her.

She did not get a chance to say the same words to him as his ardor grew once again.

Pat tried not to feel dejected the next morning, reminding herself that what Blaise had said was true. Nothing should be left undone, even though they probably had lost the Canadian government's pledge for thirty million dollars. It was still the Eagle, still Roger's dream, still her goal. Perhaps they would find new funding somewhere else. Blaise had worked one miracle, why shouldn't they try for two?

Blaise was strangely quiet beside her during the morning's ride and she wondered if he was thinking about leaving soon. She took in his handsome, well-developed frame, which filled out his three-piece blue-gray suit so well. She would not allow herself to think about the time when he would leave, even though she knew it had to be soon. She had never known him to spend more than a month in one place, and he had been with her almost two. Two months had slipped away as if in a dream, she thought sadly, then shut her mind to it completely.

Pat put on a brave face as the car came back to the same place where they had seen their hopes go up in smoke yesterday. The Eagle, a light blue bird perched on the runway, stood at attention, waiting to pass its final test, as if it did not know that now it was all for naught.

Over to the left stood Blair Afton, who was conferring with Blakely, the Canadian representative. Pat was more than a little surprised to see the men there, especially Blakely. She glanced at Blaise but got no enlightenment there.

"What's going on?" she asked.

"Why don't you go over and find out?" Blaise suggested mildly, as if she were asking about the weather.

"You're behaving very oddly," Pat said as she walked quickly to Blakely, pulling her fur parka around her. The wind was cold, she thought.

"A man in my position is never odd," Blaise called after her, "only eccentric."

She knew then that something was indeed up. Why didn't he tell her when he was arranging things? It would take all the worry out of her life, she thought, then reproached herself. Here she was, hoping and building castles in the sky again.

"Good-morning, Mr. Blakely."

"I certainly hope it *is* a good morning, Mrs.

Hamilton," he replied politely, his thin face wreathed in smiles.

He certainly looked happy for a man who just lost a contract for a factory, she thought.

Blakely thrust an envelope at her and she looked at him quizzically as she took it.

"It's from the Prime Minister," he said.

"Condolences?" she asked archly, taking her time in opening it.

"Hardly," he replied. "He had it flown here right after Mr. Hamilton spoke to him."

Pat turned to look at Blaise, who had joined her. On the field behind them, Sam was issuing last-minute orders to the pilot and to the crew, which was giving the Eagle its final check-over.

"What did you have to do with this?" she asked Blaise.

"Why don't you just read it?" he said. "I've never met a woman who asked so many questions," he said to Blakely, who nodded politely, obviously not sure of an appropriate response.

Pat looked down at the envelope. She looked at Blaise, her eyes wide, and then at Blakely. The postmark read "December 32nd."

"Still makes it within the year, doesn't it?" he asked politely, clasping his hands behind his back and making rather a grand show of looking at the aircraft.

Hurriedly, Pat took out the letter. " 'This letter was carried aboard the first flight of the Hamilton Eagle, which took place on December thirty-second of the year . . .' " Pat read no further but threw her arms around Blaise's neck, her parka hood falling away and her hair coming loose. "Oh you wonderful, wonderful man! Why didn't you tell me?"

"I've been telling you I was wonderful ever since I arrived," Blaise said in mock surprise.

"You know what I mean! This!" she cried, waving the envelope and letter in front of him.

"Oh, that. Well, the Canadians don't want to lose all those extra jobs, you know. And the Prime Minister's already gone on record saying how he's picking up the economy and preserving good relations all in one sweep. He wasn't about to toss that away, now, was he, Blakely?" he asked the man's back.

Blakely had the good grace not to turn around. "No, sir," he agreed.

Then Blaise explained, "And I didn't tell you about this because I wasn't positive it would work. I just couldn't chance setting you up for another bout with shattered hopes."

Pat was speechless for a moment, then ran over to Sam with the document and said excitedly, "Well, let's get this aboard!"

The look on Sam's face indicated that he thought something else had gone wrong, but one glance at Pat's beaming expression was all that was necessary to lay aside any such thoughts.

"Here!" she cried, shoving the letter into O'Toole's hand. "We're still in business! Sam, we got a one-day reprieve!" she exclaimed joyfully. "Fly, you wonderful bolt of cloth and glue, fly!" she instructed the plane, patting it fondly.

"I think it needs the pilot to do that," Blaise said, taking Pat's arm and pulling her back out of the way.

Pat laughed and cried as she watched the final

test go off without a single hitch. The craft was approved and it was a toss-up as to who cheered the loudest, the crew, Blakely, or Pat. Only Blaise seemed to maintain his composure.

"Well, you got your wish," he said almost calmly, smiling at Pat's exuberance.

He was going to tell her good-bye right here and now, she thought suddenly, seeing his quiet mood. Was this how it was to end? On the field of victory? Somehow, the euphoria of that victory faded quickly. But she was damned if he was going to see her break down and cry.

"Yes, I got my wish," she echoed. "At least part of it," she could not help but add.

"What's that supposed to mean?" Blaise asked, leaning over toward her ear to make himself heard over the din of the engine and the shouting crew members who were still congratulating one another.

But Pat merely shook her head, refusing to elaborate.

"Are you going to play coy now, after all we've been through together?" he asked.

Still she could not bring herself to ask him to stay. It wasn't right and it wasn't the way she wanted him to remember her.

"C'mere," he said, taking her elbow and pulling her away from the others.

"Oh, Mrs. Hamilton, it's going to be absolutely wonderful!" Blakely enthused, grabbing her hand and shaking it heartily. Somehow, she managed to smile at him and answer back while retrieving her fingers. Nothing was going to be wonderful ever again.

Blaise led her back to the car, safely out of

everyone's way. Champagne was being uncorked right in the middle of the field and even the Eagle got a dose of it.

"Did you ever wonder why I didn't get married?" Blaise asked quietly.

She did not understand why he was asking her this. He was probably going to follow it up by saying that he could not take long attachments. She looked down at the ground, willing herself not to cry or let him see the tears that were welling up inside. He raised her head to get her eyes level with his.

"Well?" he asked, still waiting.

She shrugged. "Why tie yourself down to one woman when the world is your playground?" she said bitterly.

"A grown man doesn't want a playground," he said, his voice serious. "But neither does he want to settle for second best."

She looked up into his eyes. Something in his voice compelled her to take serious heed of his words. This wasn't just a wonderful parting speech he was offering her—was it?

"You still don't understand, do you?" he asked, and she shook her head, her honey-brown hair hitting both cheeks. "As unsophisticated as it sounds, I fell in love with you the first time I saw you, looking so young and beautiful on Roger's arm. I hated him at that moment, I hated him for having seen you before I did. Yet, he was my cousin and I did truly care for him, so I did the only thing I could. I got out of the picture entirely. That was why I couldn't bear to stay here. Seeing you and not having you was torture."

"Well, you certainly didn't pine away in a monastery," she said with a small smile twisting at her lips.

"No, being a monk was not in my nature. But neither did I ever find a substitute for you—until now."

"Now?" Was there some young, nubile girl waiting in the wings who reminded him of her twenty years ago? she wondered, the tears threatening to fall. Be strong, her heart urged, be strong!

"Who is she?" Pat asked, her throat dry.

"You."

"What?"

"I was in love with the bloom on the rose, the hint of the woman to be. Now I've found that woman, and the promise did not even begin to reveal what you really are now. I can't let you go again. I might not be able to gallop to your rescue in another twenty years." He took her into his arms, holding her tightly, oblivious to the several pairs of eyes that turned to look their way. "This is not the most romantic place in the world, and if you prefer, I'll fly you to the base of the Eiffel Tower, although this might be the site of a semihistoric event in its own time."

"Are you saying what I think you're saying?" Pat asked incredulously, her heart beating madly.

"I know five languages. I can ask you in each one, as long as you give me the right answer," he said, his eyes smiling warmly at her.

"English will be fine," she said, terribly hungry to hear the words she had dreamed about.

"Will you marry me?" he asked against her cheek. "Think how practical it'll be. You won't even have to change your stationery."

She threw her arms around his neck. "I'd marry you if your name were Rumpelstiltskin!" she cried, the tears falling freely now.

"It would never fit on the business cards," he said just before he kissed her, once more bringing back the world of passion and the promise of every day being a wondrous bonus, a December 32nd.

THE EDITOR'S CORNER

Delightful. Good old Webster says that delightful describes "That which gives keen lively pleasure to mind, heart, senses." So, there was no other word I could possibly use to sum up how your reception of *LOVESWEPT* has made all of us who work on the series feel. Your warm, enthusiastic notes and letters, along with the generous remarks of reviewers, have been truly *delightful!* Our authors join me in thanking you for the keen lively pleasure that your response has given us.

Next month's *LOVESWEPT* romances reflect the brilliance of the July days when you'll be reading them. They shimmer with emotion, sizzle with romance! All three authors live in sun-drenched California. What a coincidence—or is it?

HARD DRIVIN' MAN (#10) by Nancy Carlson doesn't have just the hero in the driver's seat of an 18-wheeler, but also the young and lively heroine. And a more feminine truck-driver heroine you can't imagine. This is a fiery and truly exciting romance . . . and how it made its way into my hands may interest you. A little over a year ago I gave a workshop for prospective *LOVESWEPT* authors in southern California. Emphasizing that fresh elements were essential in our love stories, I mentioned that, for example, no one had ever sent me a romance featuring truck drivers. Further, I commented that I'd read an article about several charming women who are successful in this job. Well, about a week after I got back to my office, **HARD DRIVIN' MAN** arrived in the mail with a note from Nancy's agent clipped to it. The note read, "Ask and you shall receive!" Now, I wonder, what other marvelous

(continued)

areas are being neglected because I haven't thought of them and asked? I'd love to hear from you about occupations, settings, and so forth that you feel are bypassed and you would like to see in our romances.

BELOVED INTRUDER (#11) is in the tradition of Noelle Berry McCue's highly popular love stories! It is a romance of searing and intense emotion, incendiary passion. I can't tell you how much respect and affection I have for Noelle. This novel was created during a period of great stress for her because of illness in the family. Not only did she come through with a riveting book, but she came through on schedule. She's a real pro and a lady with real courage.

We are sincerely pleased to be able to publish Joan J. Domning's first book, **HUNTER'S PAYNE** (#12). There is a matchless incandescence of feeling in this romance. As editor I go over a *LOVESWEPT* romance at least four times, the last in the galley or proof stage. And, even the fourth time through, I chuckled and despaired with Karen Hunter and P. Lee Payne . . . and believe I could never fail to respond to their moving scene on pages 177 and 178!

Happy July reading with *LOVESWEPT*!

Carolyn Nichols

Carolyn Nichols
  Editor
LOVESWEPT
Bantam Books, Inc.
666 Fifth Avenue
New York, NY 10103